Twenty-Five Years

-as a-

Fireman/EMT

Peter Skillman

D1411936

PublishAmerica
Baltimore

First printing

ISBN: 1-4137-6133-X

PUBLISHED BY PUBLISHAMERICA, LLLP

www.publishamerica.com

Baltimore

Printed in the United States of America

...Table of Contents

In the Beginning…   9
My First Fire Department   13
The Crash by the Curve at the Church   17
Fire Trucks, Tankers and Equipment Trucks   19
Crash Skillman   21
Experience   23
A Call of the Heart   26
Potter's Alley   27
Adrenaline   29
Car Accidents   31
Children's Shoes   33
Watch Out—You Know Who is Coming   35
Homer   37
The January Midnight Barbeque   38
Memories   40
The Football Game…#55 Down   43
My Eight-Year-Old Hippy Brother   45
My Dumb Cousin   48
A Car Has Hit a Child by the Skillman House   50
Play Ball   53
Crimson Red   55
Shamla (Sibling #4)   57
The Night the Dead Lived   59
1-2-3-4-5-6-7-8-9-10-Time-10-9-8-7-6-5-4-3-2-1   64
The Glory Hounds   66
The Woods   68
Uncle Sherm   72
The Kid Calls   74
Thank You for Saving My Life, Mister   76
My Friend's Kid   79

The Lost Little Boy   80

The One Who Didn't Make It   82

She's How Old?   84

Anyone Out There Looking for a New Adventure?   86

My Motorcycle Accident   88

The Night I Caught the Big One   92

Every Now & Then We Did Something Right   94

It's Never What You Expect   96

1 + 1 = 3   98

Baby   99

There's Danger Lurking Up Ahead   101

To My Drivers   103

Mutual Aid   105

24/7   107

Our Neighbors   109

Friends   110

The Parade   112

The Cockatiel   114

Fireman   116

The Day the Sky Turned Black   118

In the Navy   123

Helicopters, Jets and Planes   125

The Infants   128

The Missing Girl   132

Bingo   134

DOA   136

10-13   138

Violent Patients—Violent Families   140

What's Wrong with My Dad?   141

That's My Wife   143

Drugs   144

Humor Is a Wonderful Thing!   146

The Man That Stutttered   147

We All Gotta Have Our Fun—The Rookie   150

And I Remember When   152

You Have to Keep a Level Head as an EMT 155
Performing Under Stress 157
Animals 159
Deer 160
Speaking of Deer Inside of Cars 161
Slinky 162
Bees 163
Spiders 164
Horses 165
Hee Heee Heeelp Purrr! 166
Sleeping and the Lack of It 167
Spouse's Tolerance 170
The Wonder Years 172
Tradition and My Grandfather 175
Red Light, Green Light 177
EMTing Yourself 179
Storms 182
Floods 184
Tornados 186
Blizzards 187
Blizzards and Curves 189
The House on the Left 191
Respite Care 193
A Father's Pride and Joy 195
The Disaster Plan That Was Disastrous 197
Death on the Highway 200
Life in the Country 201
Bull 202
Life in the City 204
Life In Between 206
Life 208
The One-Armed Fisherman 209
The Do's And Don'ts of a Fireman/EMT 210
Confidentiality 213
Back to Our Neighbors 215

The Typical Everyday Run-of-the-Mill EMT/Ambulance Run   217
The Not-So-Typical Everyday Run-of-the-Mill EMT/Ambulance Run   220
The Jaws of Life   223
The 10-13 in the Creek   224
The Day the Fire Hall Caught on Fire   226
Refresher Courses   227
Patches   229
Honesty   230
My Dad Is a Fireman   232
Questions with My Answers   234
Yesterday   238
This Is the Last Story…I Promise   240

Illustrations by Sara Skillman
Edited by L. Bundy

In The Beginning...

▪▪▪

I don't know if it was the way she asked me or just that she asked me at all that sort of threw me. "Peter, would you like to go to a first-aid class with me tonight?" Mom asked me.

"First-aid class?" I replied. Why? What do they teach you to do, put on Band-aids? "Yah!" I said, trying to show a little enthusiasm.

I figured that Mom really wanted to go to this thing, and I had already seen that night's rerun of Bonanza, when Hoss fights off the entire Indian Nation single-handedly, so what the heck! I also figured out that if the rubber met the road too hard, I would have Mom there to put on the brakes and pull me out of any skid I might encounter.

It was a Sunday night, and it was just going to be a brief introduction to the course. The real McCoy, Luke, would be happening every Tuesday and Thursday night throughout the winter.

What I didn't know was that, in her own way, this was Mom's plan to pass on to me the attributes of caring for others. I had already learned many things from her as I watched her care for us six kids: four boys and two girls. Seeing how I'm writing this book, I can say I was the best looking of the bunch.

Mom's caring was not just limited to the Skillman Clan. Also included were the neighbor's kids, relatives, stray dogs, cats, and basically anything that was moving and breathing. She once found an injured four-foot-long black snake that was taking up residence in our basement. She cared for it by feeding it mice from mousetraps.

She provided it with cups of milk also. Well, the snake recuperated. Mom was so proud of her accomplishment that she brought the thing up the cellar steps and into the living room to show everyone. It took about three weeks to unpeel Dad and me from the living room ceiling. *I hate snakes*!

Mom's caring traits were more often of the routine kind such as fixing up scraped knees and the normal run-of-the-mill bumps and bruises. However, life did offer her many emergency opportunities to prove her knowledge and grit. My mom had grit!

So off we went down to the local department. It offered me the chance to swallow my first dose of learning to care for others. Little did I know that that night would be the kickoff of what would end up being twenty-five years or more of providing care for others in one form or another.

The introduction to this first-aid course looked like a piece of cake when I first entered the fire hall. At the time, about twenty people had arrived, and more were coming through the door. I thought I could blend in easily and avoid being called on. I didn't want to impress everyone with my vast amount of knowledge on our first meeting. I detested being called on, as was too often the case in my eleventh grade English class where most of the answers still remain a mystery to me.

Mr. Thompson was to be our instructor. He was a full-blooded Seneca Indian, and when he smiled at me, I calmed myself with the reassuring thought that the scalping of students went out after Custer's last stand. He stood six-foot-twelve-inches tall and delivered well-rehearsed lessons in a deliberate and effective manner. We were then told to take a break, and on our return we would be watching a movie on natural childbirth. *Cool*, I thought. *This will beat out Bonanza any day. Maybe next time Little Joe!*

On the ride home that night, Mom stated, "Peter, when Mr. Thompson started the childbirth movie, I wasn't exactly sure if you were going to leave the room, vomit, or continue to turn even greener!"

"Thanks for your encouragement, Mom!" I said as I slumped deeper into the car seat.

So the first day ended. Mom and I decided to complete the course. After having my first official card for one month, not killing anyone or being drawn into a multi-million-dollar lawsuit for malpractice, I started building my much-needed confidence. I at least knew half of what I was trying to do. "There is a God," I said.

As with most things in my life, I felt the need to advance rapidly. The mundane has never appealed to me. I have no qualms with "first-aiders," but I needed to find out more, especially about all that neat equipment that you would see used on those medical shows like *General Hospital* and "The Old and the Breathless"!

Both volunteer and paid ambulance services have levels ranging from the never faltering "first-aider" to the all-knowing, just-under-God Paramedics. So, through my diligent investigative skills and having a good friend tell me about an upcoming EMT course, I decided to take on another challenge and enrolled myself in this next level of caring. EMT is, of course, the abbreviation for Emergency Medical Technician.

I soon came to the realization that this course was hard! Mom was not there. She, in her wisdom, wanted me to take this flight solo, learn to soar with these eagles and not remain just a pigeon. I did pass the final exam, but not without hitting that EMT book harder than any other subject I had studied in my life. I recognized that I had now developed an intense interest in this field of study. Obtaining my first EMT card reinforced in me that this stuff is serious business and not to be left to amateurs who sit around and watch reruns of Bonanza all the time. I was proud to hold my EMT card and know I had grown.

I did not belong to a fire department. Instead, I chose to freelance for a while and not wear out my new card too quickly.

"Who made off with my fishing tackle box?" my dad said as he was staring directly at me.

"Well, Dad, we haven't gone fishing in quite some time, and I wanted to make a neat first-aid kit, and the tackle box just fit the bill," I suggested. He sort of smiled at me and thought for a moment, then said, "I don't mind if you use it, but I sure hope that you do better at first-aiding or whatever you're doing than you did at fishing."

Thanks, Dad. Encouragement was scarce around the Skillman Farm.

I went to the local drugstore and purchased various items for the kit. I bought different sizes of sterile gauzes, a few small bottles of 0.9% normal saline and, of course, tape. Oh how I love tape. Tape fits the saying, "the more, the better." When I get done taping a patient's injury in place, they end up looking more like an Egyptian Mummy with a splint.

The Pharmacist who cashed me out must have thought one of two things:

1) This guy was sent to restock the store room at the General Hospital or
2) He's a new EMT who wants to freelance and is busy filling up his dad's old fishing-tackle box with all our neat medical stuff!

I was enthusiastic, and Marcus Welby, M.D., was in for some stiff competition.

"That will be forty-seven twenty-five, please," the Pharmacist stated skeptically. I don't think I would have bought it all if he hadn't said "please."

I did have a fair amount of supplies tucked away in that tackle box. I felt that I was ready to handle anything that came down the pike. Even though I was ready for a major car accident or your occasional plane crash, nothing was coming down the pike! I was becoming more anxious as the days passed.

Dad saw this change in me and said, "Why don't you go up to the fire hall and put in an application to join? Seems like nothing's biting around here, and you might get more action there." Out of desperation and in hopes of any action at all, I filled out the application to join the fire department.

Two weeks later, I was voted in at our area fire department, and I became a full-fledged member. This department, as most rural departments are, was voluntary. I've often wondered how much support these departments would have received if, instead of reading voluntary, the sign hanging on the building read, *Your Local Area Pay AS You Go Fire Department*. Just a thought, although I do believe attendance would dwindle at the next fire hall social.

The point that I'm trying to emphasize is on the word *voluntary*. That word represents countless man/woman hours of dedication freely given for the benefit of others. Yes sir, I did become a paid EMT for a year or two. Hey, a growing boy has gotta eat, but the majority of my quarter of a century of service to the public was given freely as a volunteer fireman/EMT.

Now that I've dislocated my shoulder by patting myself on the back, I'll continue on with the story.

My First Fire Department

♩♩♩

As you may have discovered by now, I am reluctant to specifically name people and places. I only mention my family members' names, as I don't fear legal prosecution from them. [None of them have yet paid their poker debts from the last family reunion.] Actually, patient confidentiality should be one of your highest priorities unless your Uncle Louie is a darn good attorney.

The first fire department I joined was to be one of the two rural departments I admit associating with. It was also the place where I was introduced to the action I craved so much. I soon learned that if I was going to stay in this sort of activity, I would have to give up the freelancing, "Lone Ranger" attitude and learn to work with others.

The fire chief said we were to have a woodsman's contest fundraiser. This so-called contest was a direct challenge to me. I thought, *this could be kind of fun, seeing how I'm sort of woodsy myself.*

After all, I did spend most of my free time as a youth playing in my great uncle's woods, and I managed to pick up a few woodsy tricks of my own along the way.

Those bits of information would prove handy now. I figured I already had these Paul Bunion wanna-bes beaten as I held that advantage.

"Sure, I'll be glad to help out," I said enthusiastically.

"Now there's a live one!" I heard someone say.

That Sunny July afternoon came, and I was ready for hunting *bear*! I couldn't wait to show off my knife- and ax-throwing abilities and win a few prizes along the way.

The turnout for that day was much higher than anticipated, and various activities were occurring simultaneously. There was a balloon-blowing contest for the young, grease pole climbing for the older kids, and storytelling for the young at heart. "Well, I remember back in '92—that's 1892…" the old timer said to his checker-playing partner.

Our fire department's grounds had a pond on it commonly known as the fireman's pond. Things didn't get too sophisticated out there! I thought it was kind of a cliché too.

One of the events going on that day on the fireman's pond was canoe racing.

I was involved in an event called "eating" at the time the event occurred. All I heard was the word "go" followed by onlookers yelling and cheering for their favorite canoeist.

For the benefit of land-lovers, a canoeist is one who paddles a canoe.

Then it happened! One of the overenthusiastic canoers paddled too hard and turned over his canoe.

"I can't swim!" he yelled. His plea for help almost went unheard as the crowd continued to cheer the others on.

Then someone else yelled, "He can't swim!" My first thought was, *What is he doing in a canoe if he can't? He's going to drown.*

I was finally attacked by my cerebral neurons hitting me all at once, saying, "Ah, hey there, Pete. Yes, you standing there with your mouth full. Now would be a good time to put your corn dog down and go help save this poor moron before it's too late."

I dropped the corn dog.

I hate to waste good food, you know. I tore off my shirt, took off the fireman's boots, and ran towards the pond.

As I was swimming toward this submerged, half-drowning fellow, I began to contemplate just exactly what I was going to do once I did reach him. I could swim fairly well but was a lifeguard by no means.

I then happened to notice another swimmer parting the waters much better than I.

He got to the almost-drowned canoeist first, and when I arrived, Moses said, "Grab underneath his arm and hold onto the capsized canoe." He continued, "It will still float, and we can all kick back to the shore together."

We used the overturned canoe as a floatation device, and slowly and calmly, we all managed to return to the shore safely. This was the exact lesson I needed to learn, *teamwork*. I know I couldn't have saved him alone. Teamwork was what succeeded that day, and I have used it ever since.

Sub note: Never eat a cold corn dog!

The Crash by the Curve at the Church

✦ ✦ ✦

I hadn't been in this fire department for even two months when I got my very first car accident call.

I was still living at my parents' house, which was located at the bottom of the second-steepest hill in our county. It was named Brockway Hill, and it was a chore getting up that sucker to reach the fire hall in the wintertime.

The whistle blew, and I first had to make a mental check to see if we had an available car that I could use to drive to the fire hall. It was a miracle. Tom and Phil, my two elder siblings had both neglected to borrow Dad's 1967 Plymouth Barracuda. It had rust everywhere, a cracked windshield and three bald tires. I'd learn later in my career that this is known as the perfect fireman's automobile.

The roads were slick as I managed to top Brockway sideways.

I knew the hall was only seconds away but shockingly came across the scene of this accident before I ever reached the hall. I was alone and on my own as the cold snow blew into my face as I exited Dad's car.

Ellery Center was a very, very small country town. The word town even seems too big to describe these two roads that intersect.

Among the listed establishments in this Town were the Ellery Center General Store, the store that my future father-in-law would soon own, a

Grange Hall and one Baptist Church. The church was located on the corner just prior to the fire hall. This was the location of this car accident; it was a beauty.

Inside the car were a man and woman. While trying to open the locked passenger car door, I heard the siren of the fire truck as it was pulling out of the hall. The man got out of the driver's side and said, "She's hurt real bad." I again looked into the car and first saw a whole lot of blood. The fire truck stopped, and I was joined by another EMT. He had brought out a large medical supply kit that held various emergency supplies, just like my tackle box that was still sitting behind the seat in the car. We called this the orange box, pretty much because it was a box and it was orange.

I then heard another fireman call for mutual aid from a nearby department, as we needed to use their ambulance. We didn't own one yet.

The other fireman/EMT unlocked the passenger side door, then instructed me to hold this gauze tight to her neck.

I did this while noticing a very nasty cut to her neck. This was where all this blood was coming from that covered everything in the two front bucket seats.

The ambulance arrived, and due to its small size, I was asked to stay behind and let the other two EMTs take care of her.

I waited with a veteran fireman until the tow truck hooked up to the crashed car and pulled it out of the ditch. The car was then towed down the road.

We drove back to the hall. While backing the truck into the hall, my veteran buddy said, "It's just about time for coffee, don't you think?"

When I finally concluded he was asking me a question and not making a statement, I responded, "Sounds good to me."

Another fact I learned quickly: Firemen and EMTs basically survive on adrenaline and strong black coffee.

I added guts and courage to my list that night as I sat my cup down and saw the four red fingerprints and one red thumbprint on that white Styrofoam cup!

Fire Trucks, Tankers and Equipment Trucks

♦♦♦

"You don't really expect me to drive that thing, do you?" I said to another senior fireman.

"Oh, you will in time," he said. He continued, "Fire trucks are big, and some water tankers are bigger. It doesn't happen overnight," he said. With a sort of big brother tone, he said, "Experience comes with time and *safety* is the name of the game. Don't ever forget that!"

Two Firemen sitting at a fire hall next to a nuclear-powered, pot-bellied stove on a cold winter night in the middle of winter, in the middle of a blizzard in the year 3012. Crash Skillman was his name, by gum! Why, I hear tell that way back when, he once drove a fire truck through a tornado. The tornado sucked all the water out of the truck, sprinkled it on the barn fire and put it out all by itself, but Skillman got so nervous 'bout that time that he crashed that empty truck into a dinosaur.

I swear I'm telling the truth! Pass that coffeepot will ya!

Pete's
No.1 Vol.
Fire Department

Crash Skillman

***

It was my very first job as a paid professional Emergency Medical Technician. I had retired from the navy after serving four years; then I found the perfect job.

It was going to be so cool. I got to wear a uniform that someone else cleaned and pressed. I didn't have to salute anyone, and I just got to enjoy what I loved to do the most: driving and, of course, EMTing.

Our home base station where we had the ambulances was located on a busy one-way street in the city. After every call, we would return to our base station and stop the rig out in front of the station. Then we would have to back up the rig while turning into the garage of this ambulance station at a ninety-degree angle from the road. No big deal!

The guys I was working with showed me how to do this more easily. They would just turn on the red light before backing up the rig. This would stop the traffic and allow you more time to turn as carefully as possible as not to hit anything.

"Okay, guys, I'm pretty sure I'm ready for it now!" I crowed.

They winced.

The boss wanted us to go get lunch, and as he was the owner of this business, he said, "Take Rig fifty-one, go get the pizzas and let Pete drive." His first mistake!

We went and got the food, and as we were returning, my partner said, "Are you sure you got the hang of backing the rig up and turning at the same time, Pete?"

"Sure, no sweat, Bub."

I pulled up to the garage and turned on the red lights. I checked my mirrors, and no traffic was coming, so I crept the rig backwards and drove it right into the middle of the driveway. "I did it!" I gleamed.

I then thought the boss would really think I knew what I'm doing if I backed the ambulance directly inside the garage. "Don't get out yet," I said. "I'm going to put it inside the garage, just for the practice."

I checked the side mirrors and saw that the sun was reflecting off the mirrors in a strange way.

I would have sworn on my dear deceased grandmother's grave (Mom's side of the family) that the overhead garage door was up when I backed that rig inside the garage. *CRASH!* It wasn't.

The door came crashing down, and my boss came running out of his office.

Right about this time, memories of doing push-ups in boot camp in Orlando, Florida, in one hundred degree temperature started looking pretty good.

My boss looked at the large double overhead garage door that was now lying on the garage floor and said, "Did you get anchovies or not?"

That afternoon, we all helped to rehang that door and ate pizza while the guys I worked with shared the mistakes of other rookies with me. Me knocking the door off its hinges was nothing compared to what my predecessors had achieved.

He was a cool boss, the owner of this ambulance company. I do recall him saying when the phone rang again for the first time after the falling door saga, "Pete, get in the back. I'm driving!"

Experience

***

You, the reader, will soon discover that I, the writer, have a tendency to skip around a lot on my timeline of past events. I'm sorry if this confuses you, but that is how I remember these stories.

My wife Peggy will tell you that I also have a tendency to go off on tangents! Don't believe her. Why, I remember just the other day when I went fishin' with my good buddy Vern…

Seriously, when I decided to actually sit down and write about these stories, I just started to hand-write them down as I remembered them and not in any particular order. I haven't been in any particular order since I was in boot camp, this being the pre-Navy experience!

I would also like to reveal that most of the names and places in these stories have been changed to protect the innocent, *me*!

I hate lawyers, and all of the proceeds from this book will be going to the kids, *mine*!

I sometimes picture you, the reader, sitting by a crackling fireplace or at least indoors on a bone-freezing December blizzard night with a hot cup of whatever you drink and wishing it could have been you during these exciting times.

I can remember the day when a guy couldn't swing a dead cat by the tail without hitting an EMT wannabe in those training classrooms. Nowadays, a person is doing well just to find an EMT course being offered.

I reserve the hopes of the young readers taking an interest in this field and becoming involved. I encourage the young at heart to sit back with your hot toddy or whatever and read on and enjoy *911: Twenty-Five Years as an EMT*.

By the way, if you are entertaining a hot toddy right now, don't go out and drive this evening because it's cold, wet and snowing outside, and I want to stay home tonight by my crackling fireplace, drying my socks. Cheers.

Just for your own reference point, I was first in the United States Navy serving as a Hospital Corpsman, abbreviated Hm. I was eventually at the rank of E-4, which in the Navy is called a Third Class Petty Officer; thus, Hm3.

I haven't figured out yet what was so petty about my rank.

When I was off military time, you might say on my own civilian time, I did work for an ambulance service in Portsmouth, Virginia, and gained much practical experience from them.

After Uncle Sam honorably let me off the hook—just an old sailor joke— I joined up with another ambulance service in my hometown. Back in '79, the EMT ladder was constructed differently. I was at the level of EMT III. We were permitted to start IVs and insert endo-tracheal tubes on calls. Those are tubes placed, not jammed, down a person's windpipe, also known as the trachea. The purpose is to assist a patient with breathing.

I believe they only allow Paramedics to do those skills now days.

The very first IV and endo-tracheal tube that I put in while on the street wasn't on the street. It was down by the train tracks where this man lay, fifty feet below the bridge after just jumping from that bridge. Railroad tracks have a way of rearranging a person's dental work after the jumper kisses the tracks at about thirty miles per hour!

Inserting that tube was difficult with all those knocked-out teeth being in the way.

The rest of my twenty-five years was spent with two different rural fire departments, as previously stated.

The word rural refers to being out in the boondocks, i.e. eighteen miles from anywhere. As the old man in the woods once told me, "Well, sonny, you can't get there from here!

I could go on just about any call in the boondocks, bet and win one hundred percent of the time that it would be at least twenty to twenty-five minutes until I saw another medical face after initially reaching the scene. It got pretty lonely out there.

I eventually had to stop the practice of obtaining encouragement from the area wildlife!

Gee Rocky, did you see how fast Pete put that leg splint on me? Whoooo!

***

Give Me

Give me life
And I shall live,
Give me knowledge
And I will learn,
Give me kindness
And I pledge to share,
Give me health
And I shall triumph.

A Call of the Heart

...

As all great authors do, I started this page blank. Seriously speaking…writing, you idiot!

The next story I will share is the most difficult of all my stories for me to write about. I had only been an EMT for two years when this happened. I almost called it quits after this incident, but I didn't.

This story is written for my wonderful little sister Peggy, who, in 1961, walked across our front yard and brought back to me my little yellow rubber duck.

I was still laid up in a leg cast from a car accident and confined to that long, plastic-strapped folded-out lawn chair. I was six years old, and she was three. Oh, and Peggy, thanks for the duck!

Potter's Alley

...

I had only been seeded back into my civilian and ambulance service job for about six months and felt I remembered the small city pretty well. I was born and raised in the area, and I knew all its nooks and crannies.

I had been away in the Navy for just four years, although I didn't mind having all those detailed maps I had hidden under the ambulance seat just in case I was called to a place I had forgotten about.

My partner and I had attended the same high school five years earlier and knew each other fairly well. I felt comfortable with him as a partner.

We were both EMTs, but that night would be his turn to drive and my turn to deal with and start to heal the patients in the back of the rig—another name for the ambulance.

Our town, at that time, had two ambulance services, and we would share what were known as 911 calls. These were emergency calls that would first be called into a police department, and then divvied up alternately between them and us.

It was close to eleven thirty p.m. when I said, "It's been fairly quiet; maybe we'll get lucky and not get any more calls tonight."

We had only had two calls all day long, and being of the superstitious lot that we were, it was inevitable that we were to have at least one more call before the stroke of midnight! Bad things usually happen in sets of three.

Then the red 911 phone rang. The voice said, "This is 911!" *No kidding*, I thought. I sort of knew it wasn't going to be Batman!

The policeman continued, "Your call is a beaten-up woman lying in Potter's Alley. This is 911 clear at 2331." 11:31 p.m. for all you non-ex-military personnel.

I used to appreciate them ending their reports with the time, as we needed the time to be written on our run sheet for the start of each call. By the way, all fire departments, paid or voluntary, use military time. I hung up the phone, jumped into the rig, and started to fill out the run sheet report.

Potter's Alley was not far from our base garage, and I had just finished the first two lines of the form when the rig stopped. I grabbed the orange jump box that I knew I would be using and then climbed out the side door of the rig. I looked up at the road sign that read Potter's Alley, looked down and saw my sister Peggy lying unconscious, bleeding on the asphalt. Time stood still.

The orange box slipped from my hand as I slumped to the ground and cradled my sister's head and cried.

My partner called for another rig for back up as he recognized my sister too and realized I was of little use to him.

Days later, I was told the police were there, but I never recalled them. I was told it was cold that night but never felt it. I don't remember the red lights of the ambulance reflecting off the buildings and windows, although it also happened. The world just spun by without me as I was then guarding my sister.

I failed as an EMT that night but passed as a brother!

Later, I was told that a person passing by saw a man hitting my sister. The passerby intervened and stopped the man from hitting her; he did it by breaking the man's arm.

I felt a little better after hearing that but not much.

Adrenaline

...

While still in my early EMT days in this paid ambulance service, I made the mistakes all rookies do. I would return to the home base garage and forget to check the gas gauge. My veteran partners would point this out to me, and off to the gas station we would go. We never knew when the calls would come in, so it was essential to always stay together.

It was close to noon when the 10-13 came in. The ten numbers refer to the police/fireman ten codes. It goes from 10-1 to 10-100. A 10-13 was a car accident.

Car accident calls seemed to have an entity all of their own, ranging from a bent license plate to multiple injuries and casualties where death reigns. I was driving with the lights and siren flashing and blasting.

The dispatcher's voice came over the radio and informed us that four cars had been involved in this accident and that other ambulances would be en route to the same scene.

By the end of his message, my adrenaline was pumping, and then all of my senses simultaneously jerked the ambulance sharply to the right to avoid being hit by a fire truck that was also en route to this same scene. As I was thinking about being alert for any other ambulances, I did not, until the last split second, see this fire truck coming up behind me at a forty-five degree angle to my back left side at a five-point intersection. Both he and I had our sirens on, and neither heard or saw the other.

This was the closest I ever came to dying while working as an EMT. I'm talking about inches here, at fifty miles per hour! The farm was almost bought that day.

We did arrive at the scene of the car accident, and a car was on fire. Ironically, none of the four ambulances transported anyone, as there were no injuries.

Car Accidents

⚡⚡⚡

I could write an entire book on car accidents. Hey, now there's an idea!

Do you know how many cars are in America at this very moment? Neither do I, so let's just go on with the stories!

I would venture to say that over half of my EMT calls involved a car accident. When I heard the numbers 10-13 being announced over the emergency radios or scanners, I frequently associated these two numbers as representing a form of profanity. I knew that every car accident was unique, but in some ways, they were the same as every other car accident I had ever been to. Someone got hurt, and the only difference was who and what got hurt.

When I was seven years old, my mom was taking my brothers Tom and Phil, my little sister Peggy and myself over to our grandmother's house to face yet another green bean casserole. This drive was through the winding back hills of our county, out in the country. As Mom topped a hill, I thought it strange that she was talking to God being that it was still Saturday and not Sunday. She said, "You kids get down."

Keep in mind that this was back in 1962, and seatbelts were only worn if you wanted to look like one of the guys on *Car 54: Where Are You?*

My older siblings were busy trying to get the Sugar Daddy away from my four-year-old sister, but I stopped jumping over the seats long enough to take notice of what my mother did not want us to see. I saw a VW Bug sitting in the ditch. It had a road sign pushed through its windshield. To impress on my memory for the rest of my life, I saw this road sign resting horizontally on someone's shoulders right where his head was supposed to be but wasn't! This was my first witnessed 10-13, a.k.a. car accident.

I have written about my own run-in with a car accident somewhere in this book. I learned first-hand at an early age that cars could hurt.

Children's Shoes

...

I have dedicated most of my life to the care of children. One of my first thoughts after receiving a 10-13 call used to be, I hope there are no children involved.

Autumn is such a nice time of year. The trees change color, a nip is felt in the air, the leaves are raked then the fire hall whistle blows!

Rescue 1-2-3, you have a 10-13 at the corner of this road intersecting with that road. Your time out is 10:13.

Those numbers used to wake me out of a sound sleep.

I believe it was October thirteenth. The ambulance arrived at the scene of this car accident, and we saw a mid-sized car halfway sitting in the ditch. We approached the car, and upon initial assessment of the unconscious driver, we discovered that he was in fairly stable condition, other than being unconscious, that is. As the driver could not tell us if there were any other passengers, we were then forced to begin to survey the outside area around this car. As we did our search, we started to notice shoes, a whole lot of shoes. "These are kids' shoes!" one of the higher-educated firemen stated.

Part of the front windshield of this automobile was smashed out, and my next stomach-churning thought was how many children were ejected from this car!

I'll bet my next two paychecks that the road and ditch were littered with fifty pair of children's shoes.

After searching the area diligently and finding no children, the fireman scholar reported to me that no one else was found. "I'm glad to hear that," I replied to him, and he comprehended the entire message fully!

The driver started to rejoin the conscious world as we placed a neck collar on him and began to move him onto the backboard.

"Was there anyone else in the car with you?" I asked him.

"No," he responded.

I then wanted to ask him a question to see if he was oriented. The usual orientation questions are in reference to person, place and time, but I wanted to get fancy. I tested his memory by asking, "What do you do for a living?"

He responded, "I'm a children's shoe salesman!"

Watch Out—You Know Who is Coming

...

I was at a house fire that was in our fire district, and as usual, it was located out in the country. It was, as some would say, way back in the woods.

This two-story house was cooking when our first truck arrived. We didn't waste any time with amenities. The back of the house had flames shooting out of every window on the second story. This, believe it or not, is a good sign.

When a building is on fire, the materials that are burnt create gases. These gases rise and help to refuel the fire. Having flames coming out of these windows meant that some of these gases were also getting out and away from the fire. I said some; not all were getting out.

Firemen like to do what is called vent the roof. To ventilate a roof, a hole has to be cut into the roof. This allows more of the combustible gases to escape, thus enabling the fire to be extinguished sooner.

One of my firefighting buddies is a farmer. He has worked very hard all of his life. The muscles that he carries earn him any respect that he seeks. I cannot think, off hand, of too many people that I have meet in real life that could have matched his strength. The guy's a brute! I'm so glad he's on our side. I'll call him Bubba for the sake of definition.

"Pete, get out of the way! Bubba's coming by you in the dark to place the ladder next to the…" *STOMP*. "Pete, where are ya, buddy?"

Bubba placed the ladder up against the house and was on the roof in a flash. "Pete, hand me up an ax so I can chop a hole in this roof," Bubba said as the house was burning intensely. "I can't seem to find it, but I'll...never mind," Bubba said as he started to punch the roof with his bare fist! I really saw him do this. He punched a hole right into that roof after hitting it only three times. Adrenaline or brute strength, you decide!

Hey, Bubba, let me get that for ya, buddy. Anything else I can get ya? Want a cup of coffee?

Homer

...

While walking into the fire hall one sunny day, I happened to run into Homer. Homer is a good-hearted fireman who actually did finish the sixth grade. He said to me, "Pete, you went to medical school, didn't you?"

I corrected, "Nursing school."

"Well, anyhow," Homer continued, "my wife said to me just this morning that she still has the bug, and it is still in her yet. Then Homer said with his most recently invented medical-toned voice, with a drawl, as he intently stared at me, "Where do I look to get it out of her?"

I just sort of looked at him, and with my polished medical-toned voice, I replied, "Homer, don't worry about playing doctor and just go home."

The January Midnight Barbeque

···

In the country, barns are frequently seen among the landscape. I like barns as they remind me of my youth when I spent many hours in my great uncle's barn, playing in the haymow. I also worked husking corn on the upstairs wooden floor for five cents a bushel. I spent a lot of time looking for all that candy I bought with the hard-earned money that I had hidden away in that barn away from my brothers.

This night was to be one I would not forget, not that I forget any of those fire call nights!

The air smelt of burning dry grass that winter night. *Has to be a barn fire somewhere*, I thought. I slid into my awaiting car, thinking I was so smug, knowing that grass doesn't grow in the middle of winter and a field fire was out of the question.

"We got a barn fire up at Mr. Green Jean's farm," the Chief stated as I entered the hall. "Pete, you take the small tanker, and try to keep it on the road this time," he mused in a serious but teasing manner. I inched the tanker out of the hall and immediately noticed that the ice-covered roads were still ice covered. I knew it would take a while to reach the scene, but reaching it slowly was better than not reaching it at all. I nursed it through (no pun intended) first gear and felt exhilarated by the sound of the engine. To my dismay, my forward progress was slow, and I really got ticked off when that battery-powered bunny passed me! I did manage to reach the scene before the company two counties away did. I positioned the tanker in the line of tankers that were feeding the swimming pool.

Let me explain something. In the country, when a bunch of guys get together on a freezing winter night to put out a barn fire, a metal-framed, rubber-lined holding tank is placed onto the ground. This is called the swimming pool. The tanker trucks take turns putting their water into this holding tank while the other empty trucks go get more water from a nearby creek, fire hydrant or unguarded in-ground swimming pool! Then a main pumper truck is used to suck the water out of the swimming pool and feed the water to the main hoses.

Barn fires take a lot of water to put out. Fire fighting is hot, dirty work, and sooner or later someone ends up taking a bath in the swimming pool, whether it be spring, summer, fall or winter. This is an act that is often seen as involuntary! *Aahyah, Splash*!

I set the brake on the truck and then set the wheel chuck. I smelt the air when I was outside of the truck and knew what I was smelling was beef, and I wasn't sure it was dead yet!

This 911 call had not been placed until the top of the barn was fully burning. The farmer said he was awakened by the smell of smoke. The firemen were not able to get all of the livestock out of the barn on time, and some of the cows did burn alive.

Memories

***

As I previously mentioned, my mom pretty much got me into the EMT business, and my dad got me going with the fireman part. I believe now that their intentions were to have me be prepared to handle life's situations of the unexpected nature in the best way possible. They sure had their share of them. We can all remember family accidents or unexpected situations that demanded immediate attention.

I have dedicated this book to the loving memory of my mom and dad. Please allow me to share some off their catastrophes with you. It was observing and living through these experiences that helped to prepare me for what was to come.

Mom and Dad, I can sum up all that you two did for me in three words: I love you.

The Football Game... #55 Down

♩♩♩

My oldest brother Tom was the one that I had the hardest time remembering an injury from days past. I cannot remember a childhood accidental injury, but I also know that I have to write something about him in this book, or I'm sure I'm due for a thrashing at this year's family reunion. *Ouch*!

Tom was the jock of the family. He played all the sports in high school as he was majoring in girl watching! All sports, that is, except for tennis, and he left that 15/Love to Phillip.

Tom will tell you every time he sees you that his love of football is his best memory of high school. Getting Dad's car stuck in the mud on a back dirt road while parking pulls in a close second place. *Ouch*!

It was a cold fall day when the whistle was blown. For once, it was not a fire hall whistle. The football sailed off of the tee. The crowd cheered, and the game was intense. At least that's how Tom tells it. Dad and I were sitting in the bleachers watching the game. Tom was the center for our team and hiked the ball. All eyes went to the quarterback and his throw. The play ended, and all our players returned to the huddle except for Tom. He lay in mid-field, writhing in pain. My father instinctively bolted from the bleachers, vaulted over the hand railing that separated the spectators from the playing field and ran out to his fallen son. "What is it, Tommy?" Dad inquired.

"I got hit!"

For posterity's sake, we won't mention where. A few minutes passed, and Tom was back up hiking again. Dad returned to the bleachers.

"What happened to Tom, Dad?" I inquired.

"Never mind! Just eat your popcorn!" Dad said while returning to his seat, still laughing.

My Eight-Year-Old Hippy Brother

...

Before the years of Woodstock and LSD, thrills were hard to come by. Not that Phillip or I knew anything at all about looking for them to come by in the first place at age seven and eight!

"Let's go down to the creek and see if the bear has come back," I said to my one year, four-month-older brother Phillip.

"No!" he growled. "Mom said if she ever catches us down there again without her being with us that she'd skin us alive. Then she'd sell our hides to that crazy Indian that lives down the road."

"So what are you waiting for?" I asked. "Let's go."

"No," he insisted.

"Well, how about we go over to Uncle Sherm's barn and swing by that haymow rope and then drop into the haymow?"

Phillip, in his eight-year-old philosophical teaching voice, replied, "Now if we do that again and you happen to land on the pitchfork this time, Mom will hold me responsible for the rest of my natural life; no dice!"

I soon became bored with coming up with suggestions to try to encourage this male bonding, so off I went to swing in the haymow alone after I first scouted out for any fresh bear tracks down at the creek.

No bear tracks, and my hands were now rope burned to the point where they were pink when I stopped swinging on the haymow rope. I knew I should have borrowed Dad's new white leather gloves. *I wonder if he has found them yet after we guys used them the last time when we greased our bicycle chains?* I said to myself as I came down the farm driveway hill towards our house. I thought maybe Dad was in the garage looking for them, as the garage overhead door was up.

As I came closer, I noticed my little four-year-old sister Peggy crying, Phil was sleeping on the dirt floor of the garage, and Dad was not there. Peggy's crying was an ongoing process, but why would Phil be sleeping on the garage floor when he had a perfectly good bed upstairs in the house? I attempted to rationalize but could not come up with a plausible answer.

"Peder!" My little missing-toothed sister Peggy said. "Philly is sleeping, and he won't wake up." At the age of seven, I was not a nuclear physicist. I'm not one now either, but I knew then all was not right at 523 Bemus-Ellery Road.

"Hey Mom!" I yelled as I came sliding in through and past the front door of our house. "You better go see what is happening to Phil in the garage!" I spoke with a wobbly tone.

"What is he up to now?" Mom inquisitively probed, as she was busy doing twelve million things all at once. This is the norm for most moms, or so I'm told! *Well, Mom, if I knew, I wouldn't be running in here to get you, now would I?* I thought, but was smart enough not to actually say out loud.

"Ah, I don't know, Mom, but he's lying on the dirt floor of the garage sleeping, and he won't wake up, even after I pinched him real hard!" I giggled.

Mom was not an Olympic hurdler, but you would have thought she was practicing to be one that day. She straddle jumped past me, sprang over the dog, then vaulted the couch and sprinted around the guinea pig cages. Actually, they, the guinea pigs, lived in plastic laundry baskets. We had about twenty of them, and thanks for wondering.

Mom was out to the garage in just under record time.

Decades later, when Mom was telling us about the garage story, she reminisced, "I first saw the red five-gallon can of gas next to your brother…" Family reunions are such a wonderful thing.

"He wasn't responding when I tried to wake him up either," Mom said as she gave Phillip one of those looks that only Moms can perform. You know the look—the one that almost makes your heart stop beating!

"I never did figure out how he got that awful bruise on his cheek, but anyways, I rushed him down to the doctor's office in the village, and he finally came to. We figured out that he was smelling the gas fumes from the gas can, God only knows why!" Mom punctuated. Then she said, "I never understood why he couldn't play safely with Peter when they went down to the creek or over to the barn."

My Dumb Cousin

...

In 1964, the Beatles were still busily invading America while my cousin and I were still busily invading the back yard to make yet another adolescent-style homemade tent.

This so-called tent was essential if we were to carry out our plans. Braving the harsh elements of a clear blue sky in the middle of July with a temperature of seventy-one degrees, we hoped to sleep outdoors overnight in the back yard.

We also would make a fire pit for our campfire that was lined with creek rocks. We could take the leftover round rocks and push them over the nearby cliff, as we also enjoyed the sounds of those "Rolling Stones!"

"Hey Pete," my dumb cousin said, "Let's not throw that old blanket over the clothesline this time. I got a new idea."

I replied to my cousin, "What now, Sigmund?"

"No really!" he said. "Let's take that new eight-foot-long two-by-four that your dad got at the lumberyard yesterday and nail it to those two locust trees over there." He continued to stammer. "Then when the Indians come and attack us tonight, we can take these neat orange-colored jackknifes that your Grandpa gave us yesterday, the ones that your mom doesn't know about yet, and we can cut up that green two-by-four to make firewood so we can take down the blanket, throw it over the fire and make smoke signals to call for more help to fight off the Indians!" he finished.

Now I ask you, did I exaggerate when I called him dumb?

I must have been having a low IQ day, as the next thing I did was start to nail that green two-by-four to those locust trees. So who was the dumb one now?

We got the blanket over the board, and I would never be able to explain the reasoning behind what he did next. My cousin placed a lawn chair next to the locust tree and climbed up onto the two-by-four board.

"Watch this!" he said as he proceeded to walk across the board like a tightrope walker. I have to hand it to him, he did get halfway across the board before it started to wobble, causing him to fall four feet to the ground. He stood up, and something just didn't look right. His arm was bending in the wrong place.

The sound that followed was like that of a screech owl. He began to yell, and at about that time, Mom came running out the back door.

I had only two thoughts on my mind at that moment: One, tell Mom exactly what had happened, so she doesn't blame me. Two, don't let her see those jackknives.

Mom had not, at this time in her life, taken any training in first aid or anything, just "M.O.M. 101." So, in her wisdom, Mom instinctively felt for Sigmund's pulse at his right wrist and felt none. She picked him up. He was only six and weighed all of forty-five pounds—forty-five and a half when it rained—and she put him in the car and drove off. She didn't tell anyone where she was going, and we didn't have time to ask.

Mom drove my dumb cousin to the village doctor. After doing a quick assessment, he called the hospital that was ten miles away and arranged for immediate surgery, as my cousin had broken a bone in his arm that had somehow stopped the blood flow to his right hand.

Mom's quick thinking and her quick actions were credited for saving my cousin's hand from having to be amputated.

Mom never got any medal or award, but news travels fast in small towns, fast like a dry grass fire. The word was out on Mom, and people seemed to come to her in droves asking for free medical advice, whether or not she thought this cut was infected or not and just about any information they could get that pertained to an injury.

Night fell as I stared at the twinkling stars and said, "That dumb bell! Now I'll have to sleep outside tonight all by myself. Sure hope those Indians don't show up!"

A Car Has Hit a Child by the Skillman House

⋯

Thinking back forty-three years ago, I'm positive it was January second at exactly four thirty-one in the afternoon.

Yeah right. As my oldest brother Tom would say, "You can't remember anything. It was four-thirty two in the afternoon."

We three boys—Tom, Phil and I—used to argue about whose turn it was to get the mail from the mailbox. The mailbox was located on the opposite side of the road, directly across from our house. We all three felt quite mature enough to handle the task, being the ages of eight, seven, and five. I was five and still the best looking of the bunch! Well, after much debate, I decided that today was going to be my turn.

We lived in the country and had a rural mail route. Ours was P.O. Box 523.

Tom and Phil, if you're reading this book, I won the bet at the last family reunion that our phone number at our old house was 386-4349 and our post box number was 523, so pay up! What do you mean I went off on another tangent, Peg?

Anyways, the mailbox was on the other side of the road, and the mailman's car came and went.

"I'm going to get the mail," I told my eight-year-old brother Tom. I crossed the road, after looking both ways, got the mail, and just before starting back, saw a car coming. I waited. The car came to within thirty feet of me, stopped, and the lady driving waved for me to cross the road.

Not on your life, lady, I said to myself. Mom taught me to always wait for cars—they're bigger!

This lady was insistent and waved at me in a way that told me that if I didn't go across the road, I would be in bigger trouble, so I went. So did she. I don't know why she went, but she did.

After taking physics for about a week many years later (I dropped that class), I did learn that two pieces of matter could not occupy the same space at the same time.

POW! The Cadillac bumper hit my right leg, and as my brother Tom told me years later, "Yeah, it was pretty cool! The car hit you and sent you flying about twenty feet into the air. You came back down and landed on your head! Good thing, I'll tell you, or you could have really gotten hurt!"

My poor mother! Can you imagine your oldest son walking into the house and slowly saying, "Mom, you better come outside. Pete just got run over by a car."

Three days later, I returned out of the coma I was visiting. I noticed I had this big, heavy, white thing on my leg called a cast. My medical record stated that I had sustained five breaks of three different types in my right lower leg and also had a fractured skull. Besides that, I was in pretty good shape!

I spent five months in the hospital, and not to go off on a tangent, but I feel the need to share this with you. During my stay at the hospital, my first grade teacher had all my classmates buy me a treat at my Great Uncle Sherm's grocery store, located a few blocks away from my grade school. She brought these treats to my hospital bedside one day and told me everyone wished me well. She then left. There I sat with the goodies. Man, she brought Twinkies, Tootsie Rolls and about every kind of candy a kid stuck in a hospital bed would want.

My roommate, we'll call him Joey—just because it was me that was to become the menace—was foaming at the mouth looking at all that candy.

I, having two older brothers, was used to sharing seeing as how I got sick and tired of getting roughed up for not giving them ninety-nine percent of any candy I ever had. So I said, "Hey Joey, do you want some candy?" He smiled politely then unloaded me of about half of the total take. After five minutes or so of munching, Joey didn't look too good. Matter of fact, Joey didn't talk too good either.

After close inspection, I concluded that Joey wasn't talking at all or moving at all, and his eyes were stuck open.

"*Nurse!*" I yelled. "*Nurse!*" I shouted. "*NURSE!*" I screamed.

Two nurses entered our cubicle, and one said, "I'll get the doctor!"

The other one noticed all the candy wrappers and gasped, "Oh my God!"

I didn't understand why a federal case was being made out over just a few dozen candy bars and a Twinkie or two. I was also thinking that I wanted to get back all of those fireballs that Joey took, seeing how he hadn't even licked any of them yet, and he was in no shape to eat them now!

To make a long story short, Joey pulled out of something they called a diabetic coma, and then they gave him a private room with a view, away from me.

Some people get all the luck!

Play Ball

...

Finally, I was released on good behavior, being discharged from the hospital after serving only a five-month sentence. The doctors told Mom that I should not be allowed to play rough sports such as football or rugby. Hockey was out of the question, as they still feared for my fractured skull. They wanted me to keep what little brains I had left.

It was summertime. The cast, the doctors in white coats, the needles, and that green hospital Jell-O were all in my forgotten past. I wanted to play ball!

My mom had forewarned my two older siblings that if I got injured, they got injured.

Have you ever seen what kids call a Wiffle Ball? It's a plastic hollow white ball, baseball-sized, that usually comes with a plastic bat. I believe that its purpose is to allow the participants the luxury of playing a game of baseball safely. Well, we weren't going to have any of that nonsense. We threw that pseudo bat and ball over the cliff and pulled out the real wood and real baseball.

I was the catcher. We no sooner got started when my oldest brother Tom took a full swing at the pitched ball from Phil, and I moved up towards him to catch the ball. What I caught was that baseball bat, in full swing, on the right side of my forehead.

I still got the scar to prove it. The lights went out, and the next thing I remember was seeing that doctor in the white coat again, back at the hospital. He had a needle in his hand, and the green Jell-O was still sitting on the hospital stand! Good grief!

Sub Note: I now live in a quaint little village named LeRoy, New York. This was the place where Jell-O was invented. Figure the odds. I have also recently learned that Bill Cosby will be visiting LeRoy this summer. He's the spokesman for Jell-O, and I hope he enjoys my book!

Crimson Red

...

I was in fifth grade when all this happened. My little sister Peggy…yes, my wife's name is also Peggy, but they are nothing alike. By the way, where is she? Shopping again! Anyways, my sister Peggy and I were playing tag in the house, and I was it.

We ran all through the house and decided it was time to run outdoors. Peggy ran out the front door, across the enclosed cement-floored patio, and was going to go out the swinging glass door. It was locked. I watched her go through the glass patio door!

As stated, I was in fifth grade at the time, and we had all made valentines with crimson red paper for any heartthrobs that we may have had at the time. I often wonder what ever happened to Beatrice Elawess Garbowski?

The color of that paper crossed my mind as I watched the blood spurting out of Peggy's arm, coloring the snow on the ground crimson red.

I yelled "Mom!" louder than I can type it, and then I slumped to her side, holding onto her arm.

I would learn, seventeen years into the future, that a very close resemblance to this scene would replay itself in a similar fashion at a place known as Potter's Alley.

Thinking about it all now, I guess I could call this my very first EMT call. Phil's garage stunt was just an eyewitness report!

Even though I didn't know what I was doing, I was able to manage to slow down the blood flow from Peggy's arm by squeezing it. I did this until Mom entered the patio and said, "Oh my God!" *It must be a women's expression*, I thought, as I had heard it somewhere else before. Mom picked Peggy up and held her arm tighter than I had. An ambulance came to the house, and they both went off to the hospital.

I have reflected on these and a few more memories of past traumas to express a point. I believe that a higher power, God, prepares us for upcoming events in our lives. I think I had more than my share of prerequisites in one sense, but I also can say that I have seen more traumas in my life than most people would believe.

Shamla (Sibling #4)

See index listing under "Shammy." I mean kid calls (ha ha)

***

My mother was working at the country store in Ellery Center the night my youngest sibling, David, cut his finger. Our parents were divorced at this time. I was sixteen or seventeen and was supposed to be watching him while Mom was at work.

Most childhood cut fingers occur from a new jackknife or a piece of broken glass. Not in David's case; he had to be unique!

I forget why he had it in the first place, but David was trying to get a piece of aluminum foil torn from that roll of aluminum foil that has the really neat, sharp metal cutting edge on the side of its box. The aluminum foil isn't what got cut that night.

I called Mom on the phone. "Mom, David cut his finger real bad on a box of…it's cut pretty bad." Mom couldn't leave the store but sent a friend down to the house to take Dave to the store, so Mom could assess the situation. Dave got a few stitches that night. I got a lecture.

***

I once met a fireman from Nantucket,
Who ice fished while perched on his bucket,

The number of his catch, I then asked of him,
He looked at me and smiled, then grinned,
He said None as of yet as the Muskies
Are all that have hit,
So it should be plain to see,
I'm only fishing for the Halibut!

The Night the Dead Lived

An Unbelievable Story... But It Is True!

···

Have you ever been snuggled down in your bed on a cold winter's night and were just at that point in time when you were about to fall asleep? Me too, then that darn fire whistle goes off!

It was probably January or February. I can't remember for sure as I was almost asleep when I answered this call. It was snowing fairly steadily when I arrived at the hall.

Someone turned off the whistle before the voice on the radio said, "Rescue 123 [fake ambulance numbers], you have a 10-13 on the large hill on the town line road." Three others and I got into the rig, and the fire chief ran for his car.

Fire chiefs love moments like this as it gives them the perfect excuse to go speeding down a snow-covered road in the middle of the night in the middle of winter for a just cause and without having too many witnesses. Thanks to all of you chiefs.

A few minutes later, the chief's voice comes over the radio. "I'm at the scene, but I don't see any sign of a 10-13." Then there was about a fifteen-second pause. "Rescue 123—*expediate*."

It wasn't so much the words he used but more of the way he said them over the radio. I knew what we were going to wasn't going to be good, so I prepared myself for the worst or what I thought was the worst. When in a situation such as this, the EMT only has a few minutes to process about one hundred billion thoughts. One thought I clearly remember was that I didn't want to have to do mouth-to-mouth-resuscitation on anyone seeing as how AIDS was the latest fashion. I grabbed a piece of equipment called an AMBU-Bag. This is a football-sized soft plastic device that has an attached piece (mask) that covers the patient's mouth and nose. When the bag-like device is compressed, it will deliver needed air to a non-breathing patient's lungs when the mask is held firmly to the patient's face.

I'll need this tonight, I said to myself as we approached the scene. This is an instinct that one develops over the years. Yeah right, it was a lucky guess. As we stopped and I exited the ambulance, I saw our chief standing at the bottom of a hill down the left bank, not the Gaza strip. He yelled, "Down here!" I looked and saw four tires floating above the waterline in the field pond he was standing next to. I had the orange jump box in my hand and the AMBU-Bag was tucked inside my windbreaker. I knew I should have worn a heavier coat, but as I was running out my front door, I just grabbed the first one that was handy as I was simultaneously thinking, "Do I have my socks on?"

I should make this clear now: You don't have to be a rocket scientist to be an EMT, but a little common sense does come in handy once in a while.

Through the snow bank and down this thirty-foot hill, I ran. It was dark out, and the lights from the rig didn't shine well on this downhill angle. The chief didn't tell me that a six-foot-thirteen-inch state trooper was standing at the bottom of the hill, and when I reached him, I actually slammed into him in the darkness and almost knocked him into the pond! I said, "Oh, hi." I was a bit lost for words at that moment.

He said, "The farmer is out in the water trying to get someone out of the car."

Before I go any further in this story, I would like to point out that the real hero in this story was that farmer. He is the one that heard the crash and called in the accident. He ran down to the pond and swam out to the car. He swam inside to enter the car, cut the seat belts, and…here's where I come in.

I waded out to about my armpits when that very strong farmer literally threw a person to me. The water splashed, and when I realized what had just happened, I was able to focus my eyeballs and see that this person floating in front of me was pretty much dead. I flipped him completely over on his back, and as I started to drag him towards the shore through the water and thin ice, I was able to feel his neck area to assess for a carotid pulse, which he didn't have.

Now, I'll tell you what happened next, but don't pass it around too much—I don't want to get into trouble. In CPR class about one hundred years ago, they used to teach a maneuver called the Precardiac Thump. This maneuver is done when the EMT, couldn't have been me, takes his fist and strikes the patient's chest in an attempt to kick-start the heart. Keep in mind that it was dark and that state trooper was a good twenty feet away. He may have heard an abrupt splash of water or not; I don't know, and I never asked him. Anyways, the patient began to cough and started to talk. I pulled him to shore and delivered him to that nice (*dry*) state police officer, and I told that cop, "I'm going back out to help the farmer get back in."

I thought, *He must be getting pretty nippy right about now!* as he had been in longer than I had. The Antarctic was looking warm right about that time. Unbeknownst to me, while I was thumping and bumping in the night, the farmer had reentered the car. I no sooner got to about six feet away from the car than Mr. Farmer throws me another dead guy. Two for the price of one, a winter special. This guy was big. I may or may not have tried my little thumping secret on patient B, but I soon found out that he wasn't going to be coming out of the woods as smoothly as patient A did. After an eternity of wading through chilly water with him, we finally reached the shore.

Remember that football-like toy I had tucked away in my windbreaker? Well, I whipped it out and began to do some aggressive CPR on this gentleman. In about two minutes, patient B and I were no longer friends, as he regained consciousness and started to fight against my efforts. Now that's gratitude for ya!

By this time, some of the other fire boys had reached the edge of the pond and took Mr. B up the hill on a basket stretcher. I, feeling like a popsicle, tried to make up my mind whether I wanted to reenter the water again to help the farmer or just stand there and shiver. I suddenly turned, and the farmer was standing next to me, saying, "Lettt's gggeeettt oouutt oofffhheerree." I didn't put up an argument or make fun of his chattering seeing as how he was much larger and a little stronger than I was. (Where's Peg? She would say, "A little stronger!?")

During the time I was having my late-night winter swim, the chief had called in a helicopter to airlift one of the patients off to the hospital. As I reached the top of the hill, the down draft from those helicopter blades hit me, and I was not a happy camper at that moment. They loaded the other patient into the rig, and off he went to the hospital with a dry EMT. I crawled into the chief's car and got a ride back to the fire hall. I can't remember that fire hall feeling as warm as it did that night.

We firemen have an awards ceremony every year, and the boys wanted to make sure that I was there. They kept telling me how fun it was going to be giving so-and-so a booby award. I thought that they were going to give me a plaque with a piece of the back taillight glued on it. I had recently broken this light while backing up a fire truck into the hall. Don't let the Motor Vehicle Department know though; it will be our little secret.

Peg and I went to this awards ceremony, and after the initial ha ha's were done, the Chief said they were now going to give out the EMT of the Year Award.

"Pete get your butt up here," or some close facsimile of that were his exact words.

It still hangs on my wall next to another fireman award I received a few years later. They didn't forget Mr. Farmer. He also got a civilian award.

Over the years, when I look at that award, I try not to think of that cold night I spent saving two lives. Instead, I think of the happy memories, friendships, and the time I spent with my friends, pals, and brothers. I think of that night of the ceremony and how close we all grew together through a combined effort that had a very positive outcome. We had a lot of fun that night.

1-2-3-4-5-6-7-8-9-10
-Time-
10-9-8-7-6-5-4-3-2-1

...

Time is a strange awareness. Time is a stranger awareness when you're on an ambulance run flying down the highway at ninety miles per hour.

From the time the whistle blows until the time the rig is backed into the hall, time will do many peculiar things.

First of all there is never enough time. As you hurry along on an emergency call, it will seem as though you are never going fast enough to catch up to time.

During the ride to the scene of a call, I found myself watching the clock that hung on the back wall of the rig. I did this just to make sure that the hands on the clock weren't spinning twice as fast as normal, as it often seemed. They would do this if you didn't keep an eye on them.

You will think, *If I would have only gotten here sooner I may have been able to save his life.*

Time has a way of standing still. I have experienced this phenomenon many times. Some people will call this experience shock; I call it time standing still.

Time can also slow down to milliseconds. An example I recall very plainly is the time I was thrown from my motorcycle after hitting a moving car. I remember spinning upwards about twenty feet through the air and listening to the bird that was passing by exhaling slowly, very slowly.

Time can reverse itself. The doctor's asking me, "Was he wearing his seat belt or not? Did his chest hit the steering wheel? Where was this little girl sitting in the car when the impact occurred?" Some people of greater intelligence refer to this reference of time as memory. I would just rewind the clock and play this traumatic scene over again in my mind, then give the report.

♩ ♩ ♩

Time is expensive, and I never seemed to be able to afford enough of it.
Time is a series; The last time he had a heart attack…
Time is futuristic; The time will come when children are not left alone!
Time is a mystery, What time did the swarm of bees sting him?
Time is a gamble; I'll get to that bleeding artery in time.
Time is irreversible That shouldn't have happened this time!
Time is inevitable, His time has come!
Time is at present—It is time to move on.

Well it is about time!

The Glory Hounds

On my first date with Peggy, I made the mistake of saying, "So, did you see my picture in the paper when I was on that ambulance call last night?"

She replied, "No." I could tell right off that I was making progress!

Peggy's father owned a country general store, which is where she was working and is where our first encounter occurred. One of the items he sold at his store were newspapers. The papers he didn't sell were moved to the back of the store, and at that time, he was *storing* approximately two and three-quarters years worth of papers that rested in the far back corner.

After I had left, Peggy went mowing through every one of those papers looking for a picture of me. I believe that in her mind's eye she was picturing an eight-by-ten glossy print of my handsome face on the front page.

[Two Days Later] "I looked through a few papers (628) and couldn't find your picture; are you sure it's in the paper?" Peggy inquired as I strolled into the store and headed straight for the pop machine.

"Sure, it's right here," I stated as I turned to page twenty-nine of the paper from three days ago and pointed out the picture of my right hand pushing the stretcher. She was not impressed!

I have often been on the scene of a call and seen local photographers from our small town newspaper snapping pictures for an article. I have also seen camera crews from Buffalo scanning the site of a car accident or a major structure fire.

It never fails. You will always, always see some glory hound that just has to walk toward the camera. He has a dire need to complete an overwhelming task: get his mug in the media.

I'm just wondering how many times I can polish that same spot on the fire truck before some of the guys catch onto what I'm really up to!

The Woods

***

I have always enjoyed the woods. The wind blowing through the pine trees is a sound that cannot be duplicated. The hundreds of years it takes to grow a tall, enduring maple tree is worth the wait to view its magnificence. When a timber rattler craws up your pant leg, Yeeooww.

The woods can be a wonderful place, but they can also be a very dangerous place. I would like to share some of the "Don'ts" that I have learned over the years while being in the woods. You may be asking yourself, *Self, what in tarnation does this have to do with him being a fireman or EMT?*

I've never been hauled out of the woods on a stretcher, so please just read on my friend.

In our old white farmhouse, we used to burn firewood for the purpose of prevention. Burning firewood in our wood-burning furnace prevented us from freezing to death in the sub-zero weather we endured in Southwestern, New York, for the nineteen years that we lived there.

I was what I called an avid—i.e. one who enjoys the challenge and returns home with both legs still attached—woodcutter.

Now, for you city slickers who have never swung an ax and think a cord of wood is a Hickory fiddle playing b-flat, let me educate you on the finer points of lumberjacking and measurements. A cord of wood is a stack of wood that has been cut into little pieces and then split into chunks called chunks. These pieces called chunks of wood are then stacked into a straight pile measuring four feet wide by four feet high by eight feet long.

To cut, haul home and store in our house, garage or cellar thirty-face cord of wood a year was not unreasonable. Temperatures of twenty below were often. A wood furnace will see a cord of wood as only a minuscule snack at those temperatures. It had an enormous hunger.

So, I was one of those guys that owned an expensive chainsaw that was acquired in an inexpensive transaction, a Stihl, naturally.

Going back to you city slickers who may not have gotten the humor of that last well-thought-out joke, Stihl is a brand name of chainsaws. Okay, you can stop laughing now!

I even had a tractor and a converted pickup truck bed that I used as a hauling wagon. It was the fashion of the times. I was set. I would drive out to the woods on the tractor as it pulled this wagon, and as I entered the woods and was enjoying the scenery, I would suddenly remember I had forgotten my chainsaw gas and bar oil! So, back home I would go. Forgetting gas has been a recurring problem in my life.

When I finally got everything I needed to start cutting, which was usually about three minutes before dusk, I decided to use a little bit of strategy on these old timbers—the trees, not me!

My plan was to cut six large trees and to fall them towards each other, so when I finally did get them cut up, I would have all that wood in a close proximity.

The plans of mice and men!

I managed to cut the first tree down without a hitch.

Now you non-woodsman, city-slicker readers might not know what a hitch is. A hitch is a semicircular metal piece of...oh never mind.

I started cutting down the second tree. Keep in mind that when I say tree, I am referring to a hard wood tree such as a maple or oak that is about three and a half to four feet across and is much bigger than a breadbox. One mistake out here can cost you your life, and it almost did that day for me!

The second tree began to fall, and it was falling at a ninety-degree angle towards the first fallen tree. *Cool*, I thought. *The two trees will be close to each other*. The falling tree crossed the first tree just at about its mid section.

Uncle Sherm

What happened next is a slow motion movie that I can replay in my head anytime I want to and be glad that I am still alive!

Falling trees can kick back towards their stumps if they fall across an already fallen tree at a ninety-degree angle and first hit said tree at their midsection.

The tree hit and shot back towards me.

Let me tell you how fast I can move with a five-ton tree chasing me through the woods. *Fast*! I dropped the still-running Stihl chainsaw at my feet, and man did I make tracks. The tree shot past my mid section at a speed that would have crushed me if it had hit me before it slammed into another huge maple just inches to my right.

I am an experienced woodcutter, and after that day, I became more experienced, and lighter too.

Another helpful hint is to always look up the tree before cutting. You gotta search it for large dead limbs that may fall on your head from the vibration of the saw cutting or from the movement of the tree.

My Great Uncle Sherman Skillman spent many years cutting trees down. He used to call such dead limbs widow makers.

Uncle Sherm

...

If you are cutting in the wintertime, check the base of the tree for any large open areas, such as in a large beech tree that could, let's say, house a hibernating bear. If a bear is found, pick another tree!

Always, always know where the tip of your chainsaw blade is. A chainsaw has the ability to perform a nasty maneuver known among woodcutters—live woodcutters that is—as kickback. With the chainsaw blade spinning quickly, it has the physical ability to jump back at you if the tip of the blade binds on something. This happened to me just once.

Fatigue is not your friend in the woods.

I had been cutting for about two and a half days…okay for about two hours, and sweat was pouring off of me. The horse flies were having a ball. Get another bite there, Wilber!

On top of all my other glorious attributes, I also wore eyeglasses, and sweat was blurring my glasses, not to mention my vision. I was hot, the horse flies were hot, and the saw blade was hot. Did you know the word saw is was spelled backwards? I just learned it too! Then it happened. The front of the spinning chainsaw blade bit into and bound with another round piece of wood that was on the ground in front of the larger log that I was cutting. I didn't even see it coming. The chainsaw blade kicked back towards my head. Lucky for me, my saw has a wrist guard on it. It's tripped by having your wrist hit this lever when kickback occurs—the saw blade stops spinning instantly. The blade stopped, but the backwards motion of it didn't.

Do you remember me telling you the chainsaw blade was hot? Of course you do.

The individual blades on a chainsaw look like a small rectangle with a point on one end.

As I walked into the house after dark that evening, my loving wife said, "Peter, Why do you have a mark burnt on your forehead that looks like a small rectangle with a point on it?"

The Kid Calls

✦✦✦

My mom had a lot of kid calls, and she wasn't even an EMT. Six of us kept her pretty busy. She used to say, "I wish I could have just one day go by without one of you kids getting hurt."

As a lot of other kids in our era did, we used to vacation up in the Adirondack Mountains. Just about every summer, we went north; of course, we had to take our parents along as we were all under the age of ten and none of us drove well; yet. We camped in an old deer-hunting place. I'll call it a cabin, but it was more like an old deer-hunting place that relatives of ours built. We went there during the off-season, July mostly. We would get so excited knowing that for two weeks we had no school and would be camping in the vast woods of these mountains.

My littlest sister Shamla—we call her Shammy, but she gets real mad when we do—ran out of our maroon-colored station wagon as soon as we arrived in the camp's driveway. Oh, you had a maroon-colored station wagon too? We used to stuff our little brother Dave down the back wheel well of ours.

Shammy started running up the sand-covered driveway towards this two-story haven.

Our relatives were neglectful in telling us that they had recently strung a metal cable across the upper driveway to keep deer hunters out.

Shammy ran smack dab into the cable and still has the scar above her right eye to prove it! We Skillmans ended up with an abundant amount of scars.

The lesson I learned from this little story was how inventive my mom always was. We had the basic first-aid kit of the times, but there was no 4.0 silk or catgut sutures in it. That's really what was needed, along with a doctor to close and suture this cut. The closest hospital was probably forty miles away, and the closest doctor was eighty miles away on some golf course, so Mom made do with what she knew and with what she had.

Shamla—I better use her real name, as she is sure to be real mad by now—as I said, cut her forehead wide open, and the blood was gushing out in buckets. Actually, it was a pretty cool thing to watch! I was only eight at the time, and good entertainment that far back in the woods was really hard to come by, seeing how I didn't drive. Yet!

Mom took an ordinary Band-aid and cut it into sort of the shape of a butterfly. Nowadays they have some fancy medical term for them. They call them butterfly Band-aids! Another missed Skillman invention!

As I was saying, she then closed the cut and very tightly put this Band-aid on in a fashion as to keep the cut closed.

Mom took Shammy to the village doctor when we returned from vacation to show off her handy work, and he said he would have left a larger scar if he had sutured it.

I learned to improvise from the lesson I learned that day.

The boys at the fire hall won't let me set a broken leg with two cut saplings anymore like Ol' Daniel B. did, but I have always remembered to use what is readily available.

Thank You for Saving My Life, Mister

...

My Wife and I adopted our first child in 1991 from Seoul, Korea. Her name is Susanna Lynn Hei Young Skillman. Susie for short, but I like calling her Scooterbugger. A year or so later, Susie was starting pre-k or the warm-up class before the seriousness of kindergarten life begins. Life was good.

The whistle blew, again. "Rescue 123, the next town over requests your assistance at a 10-13 on the south road leaving town, by the curve."

So here I go off to another car accident. Got my mind and my gear set, and we were there. A large pick-um-up truck had a head-on collision with a small car. When I jumped out of the ambulance, I saw the EMT from the next town over giving care to a woman who was lying on someone's front lawn. I found myself jumping out of that ambulance a lot, not simply just stepping out of it. Then I saw a young child in a car seat, and someone said, "Pete, over here. Hey boys, look! He even has his socks on!" I was to care for this child and hold her life in my hands.

Upon first looking down at her, she had jet-black-hair with her bangs cut straight across her forehead. *Just like Susie's*, I thought. Coming back to reality a second later, I saw that the accident had caused this child to have a nickel-sized hole right in the middle of her forehead. Oh, just to remind you, in 1986 I graduated from college and got my Registered Nurse Degree.

I knew from taking anatomy and physiology that this unwelcome hole was serious! Fortunately, it had just penetrated the frontal sinus cavity, and this child had a very good chance to survive. I did my ABC assessment and found that she wasn't breathing. I started to bag her, as we call it in the field, which is giving her artificial respirations with a child sized AMBU-Bag and oxygen. I said, "Let's load and go!" The child was already strapped into a car seat, which, by the way, is where she needed to stay, so I strapped her head down securely with tape—oh how I love tape—and off we went to the hospital.

The lady that the other ambulance guys were caring for was this child's mother. We got to the hospital, and as with all calls, I gave a report while en route, and the doctors and nurses met us as soon as we reached the back door of the hospital. Care was then turned over to them, and I thought that was the last I would see of this cute little child that reminded me so much of my own daughter Susie.

About three months passed, and I found myself at a spaghetti dinner at Susie's school. I think it was a get-together so the parents could meet their childen's teacher. I was standing in the cafeteria line waiting to get some spaghetti, as I was still growing and in need of sustenance, when I felt a tug on my windbreaker fireman coat. I looked down and saw this child who was at the south road, leaving town by the curve accident. She looked up at me with her gorgeous smile and those sharply cut black bangs and said, "Thank you for saving my life, mister!"

I almost dropped that plate of spaghetti on the floor, but I managed to set it down, and I picked her up and held her. She still had a Band-Aid-sized white sterile gauze covering part of her forehead. I almost cried. Her mother walked over and introduced herself to me, and then she thanked me for saving her daughter's life.

When I finally was able to get my food and sit down next to my own daughter and wife, I thought at that moment how precious life is and how much we all need to guard it.

Then Susie, who called me Aba, meaning father in Korean, said, "Aba, why do you have that tear in your eyeball, Aba?"

My Friend's Kid

***

Being the country bumpkin that I am, I had a dream of playing country music in a band. I am a drummer, or think I am, and have played drums for over thirty years. Back in about '86, we went to a call where a young girl had fallen out of a tree house and was not breathing. This is the kind of call where you don't waste time. A person can only go for about six minutes before their oxygen-deprived brain starts to enter the land of no return. We hustled.

As luck would have it, the rig pulled into the driveway of my friend's house. He was the guitar player and leader of the country band that I was presently playing with. "Pete, she's not breathing!" he said. I did my usual assessment, quickly, and then started to perform artificial respirations. She was not responding as we headed off towards the hospital. My friend insisted that he be allowed to ride along in the ambulance. Let me tell you something. When you have one of your best friend's daughter's life in your hands and he's sitting right next to you, the cooker is turned on full blast.

We were about halfway to the hospital when his daughter opened her eyes. The look on her face silently stated, "Pete, what are you doing? Would you please get that green football-looking thing off of my face?" She began to breathe and had a full recovery.

Every time we played out with the band after that call, she always spoke to me in a different tone, and so did her dad.

The Lost Little Boy

***

"Your ambulance and manpower is requested by so-and-so's woods on Lost Trail Road to help search for a nine-year-old boy. More details will be given to you at the scene."

The more details at the scene that we received were that this nine-year-old boy had been missing in a woods the size of Oklahoma for over two hours, and he was known to be a confused child.

Upon our arrival, we were joined by about five other departments. I was guessing that over sixty people were now looking for him. The month was November, it was now four-fifty in the afternoon, and we were running out of what gloomy sunlight that we did have. The boy was also known to be wearing only jeans, gym shoes and a t-shirt. The temperature was less than forty degrees, and it was getting colder fast. We had to find him soon, or he would most likely freeze to death that night.

We were using four-wheel ATVs but to no avail—no one found him. Pickup trucks were searching the fields and any accessible area they could; everybody else was walking. We were calling his name out over battery-operated megaphones. He didn't answer! We didn't know it until the very end, but a little white poodle dog accompanied this little boy. Luckily, the dog became hungry and started to walk home out of the deep woods.

The news came over one of the guy's radio like this: "This here is Billy Bob Joe Ray Clem Albert Harmen T. Washington. [Fake name, his last name was Smith.] I see the little boy walking out of the woods. He's walking behind a little white dog."

The One Who Didn't Make It

♥♥♥

"Dad, take us down to the school parking lot so we can ride our bikes," Susie said to me on a bright summer day. So, I loaded up Susie and Stefan's bikes, and off we went.

Stefan is our second adopted child. He is originally from the country of Bulgaria. His full name is Stefan Peter Lynn Skillman. Kind of catchy, don't you think?

We hadn't been in the empty school parking lot for ten minutes when we heard the fire whistle start to blow. It was a Saturday, and I figured that not too many firemen would respond to a Saturday morning call. I was right. The whistle kept blowing, so I decided to run the kids back home and answer the call. Just as I was loading the bike back into my little blue pickup, I saw one of my fireman friends racing past the school with his blue light flashing. He saw me and was waving for me to follow him.

This can't be good! I thought. I never speed when I have the kids with me, so I just started to drive in the direction he went. It started to look like a parade when I was being passed by at least ten other fireman that were also on their way to this call with their blue lights flashing. Then the ambulance came up behind me, and I pulled off the road to let them by; it's the law you know.

As I was driving, I said to Susie and Stefan, ages seven and eight, "When we get to where the ambulance has stopped, I want both of you to stay in the truck."

"Okay!" Susie said. "You just don't want us to see any of the gory stuff." The kids had heard enough about ambulance calls to know they weren't pretty. She was right; I didn't want them to see the gory stuff.

I topped the hill, saw all kinds of lights flashing and pulled the truck off the road. A lady fireman; should I call her a fire chick? I don't think so. Not unless I want to lose a few teeth. Anywho, she came up to my truck and said, "Pete, I'll watch your kids. You'd better go up and see what you can do."

I would trust my kids entirely with any of the fire *personnel*, but that is not what bothered me at that moment! What was awaiting me up ahead did!

To encapsulate this whole picture in a word, I would say gory. A boy that had been in Stefan's class at school had run across a major road and had been struck by a car going at least fifty miles per hour. The driver was heard to say that he never saw the boy, as the sun had glared his vision. I believed it, as I later found out he was a minister.

I approached the scene, and the boy was lying in the ditch. Another EMS person and myself performed CPR on this child all the way to the hospital. The boy died.

I knew this little boy, and I knew he was in Stefan's grade at school.

When I returned home after that call, I went and held my son in my arms tightly for a long, long time.

This call bothered me. I found myself neglecting to go to any more calls for about six months. When an injury, physical or emotional, cuts very deep, it takes a long, long time to heal, no matter who the patient is! "Doctor, heal thyself," I often heard my grandmother say. She was a nurse for forty-five years!

♪♪♪

I also have an eight-year-old daughter from Thailand. Sarah Joanne Panthapa Skillman is her name. I will never hear the end of it if I don't include her emergency in this book also. Yesterday, she fell and scratched her knee, and I put a Band-aid on it. There you have it! Cured!

She's How Old?

♪♪♪

It never fails; just about whenever I was called for mutual aid to another department, I knew something would be out of the ordinary.

"Rescue 123, your ambulance is requested for mutual aid to another fire hall." Now I ask you, what kind of a deal is this? If the call was at the fire hall, and I knew this department had its own ambulance and EMTs, then what was up?

We arrived at their hall, and I saw two kids and a fireman standing outside of the fire hall. One of the kids was holding her arm with her other arm; the other child was watching the fireman snap his suspenders.

"She's got a busted arm," the fireman stated abruptly when he forced himself to stop snapping his suspenders, which allowed him the ability to speak while still standing without tipping over.

I could tell by his vocabulary that he wasn't a neurosurgeon and probably not one of this department's EMTs. She began to cry, and as I started to treat her, I asked the fireman, "Do you know where her parents are?"

"Nope." How he had a way with words! "I do know she is only twelve years old roughly."

Where this fire hall's EMTs were, I hadn't a clue. I just knew I had an underage female patient with a possible broken arm, and the parents were nowhere to be found. It never fails!

After stabilizing her arm in an air splint and calming her the best I could, I knew that I had to call the county central dispatcher and report to him that I was going to transport this underage female patient unaccompanied by a parent.

In a case like this, the EMT has to report their location, the mileage on the ambulance's odometer, and the time they left the scene en route to the hospital. That way there is some proof of how long and how many miles were traveled to reach the hospital. This is all done just in case someone wanted to say something went on that was not supposed to have gone on. Get the picture!

I found out later her arm was broken, and I also found out about the big party the night before that all the fire boys at that department attended.

How do your heads feel now, fellers?

Anyone Out There Looking for a New Adventure?

...

You may have guessed by now that one of my motives for writing this book wasn't to get on the best sellers list. Instead, I'd like to try and interest the readers, at least a few of you, in possibly wanting to become an EMT, volunteer fireman or both. Okay, the secret's out.

When I started in this profession about twenty-five years or so ago, I remember there being plenty of guys and gals at those EMT classes. In the year 2005, four years after the Space Odyssey, I noticed a lot of empty seats in those classrooms. So what's the deal? Did society change its way of caring for others while I wasn't looking? Have the stresses of life concentrated our thoughts to only caring for ourselves now? I agree that there is a lot more out there today than there was in 1972.

For beginners, how about AIDS? AIDS is a scary topic, but I will say that I dealt with it on more than one occasion. By using the right precautions, you too will be able to tell your grandkids about it. Secondly, *violence*. I could write a novel on that subject. The world is more violent today than it was back when The Grateful Dead weren't. Deal with it. When I was doing my thing in the early '70s, we thought, man this world is tougher now than ever. Whatever happened to Beaver, Wally and Eddie Haskell anyways? People learn to adjust.

Well, enough of my pep talk. Being a Fireman/EMT has done for me what no other experience could have. I even joined the Navy to find out for myself; *it's not just a job, it's an adventure.* I got stuck in Portsmouth, Virginia, for four years. Some adventure.

I hope you will consider this idea, and if you are interested in becoming an Emergency Medical Technician, please seek out professional help. *Smile.* No, really, seek out your local Emergency Medical Service in your community, and they will guide you to the right people. Don't worry, the white straight jackets come in all three sizes—almost gone, gone and totally gone!

To become a volunteer fireman, just go down to the closest fire department and say to the first guy you meet that you would like to join. Then sit back and watch him smile at you in a sinister kind of fashion and make sure you know where the exit door is.

I hope you will join the Fireman/EMT team. I guarantee you that it will be an experience that you will find nowhere else and also one that you will never forget!

Thank You!

Okay, let's get back to the stories…

I went fishin' with my ol' buddy Coley just yesterday, and he caught this 35-ton whale that jumped right into the boat and.…

My Motorcycle Accident

♪♪♪

Have you ever found yourself in a predicament that you would rather have not been in? Me too, and more than once! I'm jumping back to the years that I was in the Navy. As stated, I was in Portsmouth, Virginia, serving shore duty for four long years. My next older brother, Phillip, was on the USS *Pueblo* at the time, and I couldn't buy my way onto a ship. I was stuck in the sand!

I decided to use this opportunity to my advantage. I got really daring one day, and I went out and bought a motorcycle! They are hard to ride while on a ship, I'm told, and storing them in your ship locker is a task that becomes a bit tedious. Take note that I didn't know how to ride this motorcycle, *yet*.

"Why sure you can learn to ride it!" the salesman said as he watched me drooling over the 500cc blue metallic Yamaha. I wasn't ready for a Harley, yet.

"Okay, I'll get it!" I said to him, and that day I learned how to ride, more like balance, a motorcycle in the back parking lot behind the bike store. When I felt sure that I could drive it back to the base, I left.

I spent hours in the empty back parking lot on the base honing my driving skills. I stayed pretty much to the back roads the first three months I rode until I felt absolutely confident.

I decided to go down to Virginia Beach on a sunny summer day, and I was taking the bike. I also owned a '72 Camero, but balancing that on two wheels was no longer a challenge. (Don't believe everything you read in this book!)

The traffic was light that day as I drove along at fifty-five miles per hour. I was traveling the speed limit when time suddenly slowed down to milliseconds. I saw this dark blue Ford slide through the stop sign. My brain was beginning to tell me to jump when I realized that I was already standing on the foot pegs. When the bike hit the back quarter panel of the blue Ford, my upper legs slammed into the handlebars, and I was catapulted in a somersault fashion over the front of the bike and over the back of his car. I heard Mom's voice state, "Remember, Peter, when you fall, stay loose so you don't tense up and break any bones." Thanks for the advice, Mom!

Mom had told me these same words about fifteen years earlier. I had the bad habit of falling down the stairs all the time. Somehow she had neglected to teach me the proper technique of landing in the middle of a four-lane highway after being thrown a hundred and twenty-eight feet through the air off of a crunched motorcycle, doing a two and a half Gainer with a twist at an altitude of twenty some feet.

The world was spinning, end over end, and I knew that eventually I had to land, and it wasn't going to be fun! I did manage to stay loose, and I was highly aware of the fact that I was spinning through the air.

Thud-thud-spin-turn-roll-slide. That was only the first second of the landing period. As if it happened only five seconds ago, I still remember the landing part of that accident. I hit my lower back on the highway and rolled for what seemed like a week. I heard the squealing of tires. It was an eighteen-wheeler skidding behind me as he was trying his darndest not to run over me. He didn't. Thanks, good buddy. 10-4.

I slid on my helmet's plastic face shield the last fifteen feet. I was watching this face shield disintegrate before my very eyes as I was thinking, *I hope I stop before that shield is gone because the next thing to go is my face.* Even though I'm no Rock Hudson, more like Beaver Cleaver, I still like my face just the way it is.

The first person to get to me after I finished sliding was a state trooper. "Are you okay?" he asked.

What I wanted to say to him I can't print, but I just replied, "I think I'm still alive." I asked him, "What kind of shape is my bike in?"

"It's pretty much in the shape of a pretzel," he said. There were three hundred and twelve unemployed comedians at that moment, and this clown is trying to put in overtime! "You don't want to see it," he concluded.

I noticed that the entire left sleeve of my black leather coat was gone. I heard another siren blowing besides the officer's cruiser siren, and it was getting closer. The state trooper said he had witnessed the entire accident. He had taken the liberty to call an ambulance, a military ambulance. The base sticker on the bike and my haircut were both dead—I use that term cautiously—giveaways.

The real fun started when the EMTs, actually E-2s, got out of that Navy ambulance. These clowns were sailor buddies of mine. I heard one of them say "Hey, it's Corpsman Pete!" I was amazed that these Bozos even recognized me as I lay in the middle of this highway. They handled me well. I had hit the road with my lower back and sustained what the doc called lumbar contusions. In real words, I badly scratched the bones on my lower spine, and it hurt. These buddies of mine hauled me back to the hospital on the Navy base, and after thirty-six x-rays, I was admitted to an orthopedic ward.

I had just gotten as comfortable as possible when the state trooper who was at the accident scene entered my room. He asked me a few questions, then pulled a knife out of his coat pocket. This knife almost perfectly matched one of the six switchblade knifes that I discovered in my cowboy boots after crossing back across the border into the United States from Mexico a few months prior. Tijuana, Mexico, to be exact. To this day, I'm sure those knives were planted in my boots.

I heard "Falinggggg! Is this yours?" he asked as he held my opened switchblade knife just under my nose.

Mom taught me never to lie, especially when you're laid up in bed just after having a motorcycle accident and having a Virginia state trooper waving a switchblade knife in front or your face!

"Yes, it's mine," I said. *It must have flown out of my inside pocket when the left sleeve of my coat got torn off,* I thought.

"I saw this fly out of your coat right after the left sleeve of your coat got torn off," he said. *Déjà vu*, I thought again!

"Well, you've been through enough today already," he said. He then opened the drawer to the bedside stand, closed the knife, put it in the drawer, closed the drawer, smiled and left. I feel asleep.

Besides telling you the most traumatic event of my early twenties, I do have a good reason for telling you this story. Give me a second, and I'll try to think of one! Oh yeah.

I was entirely on the receiving end of the care given that day. I recall how helpless I felt. I could not move. I did not want to move! The guys got me to the hospital, and the doctors and nurses took it from there. I vowed that day to always remember that feeling of helplessness—to realize that the patients that I would be hauling off to some other hospital on some other day would be feeling close to the same way that I felt as I lay helpless on that four-lane highway just short of the waves of Virginia Beach.

The Night I Caught the Big One

▪▪▪

Me and the guys down at the hall used to make a habit out of getting together on Saturday nights and playing cards. Mostly poker, and mostly I lost. As we sat around waiting for the whistle to blow, it did.

"Rescue 123, please." I liked it when he said please. "Assist the CX cars, CX meaning police, and cars meaning more than one at the Drink 'Til You're Drunk Bar. It seems a gentleman is striking his head against a wall of that establishment. Central out at 0123."

In other words, the cops wanted to dump some big drunken guy into our ambulance who was trying to knock himself senseless.

"I'm game," I said to the guys, so off we went into the night. Upon our arrival at the establishment, I first noticed that at least eight sheriff cars and two state officers were in attendance to this early-morning get-together with all of their red lights flashing.

It looked like Christmas in July, but I wasn't very happy about the present I was about to receive. The next thing I noticed made my heart skip. The man who was striking his head against the wall, as the dispatcher so plainly worded it, was doing just that. He was hitting the wall hard enough to knock boards loose, and he was laughing while doing it. This twin brother to Cochise was at least seven feet tall, built like an ox, and just let out of his pen, so-to-speak!

Did they really expect me to put him in the back of our little ambulance? Taking him back to the funny farm would have been my first choice!

While en route to the call, I had put on my latex gloves. A guy has to be careful nowadays. I stood in front of this gentleman, and the story of David and Goliath suddenly came to mind. He looked at me and laughed. If I were him, I would have laughed too, as the expression on my face said it all. *I was petrified*!

The police did do their part. They kept talking to him, trying to encourage him to sit in the police car cooperatively without a fight. It was apparent that Tonto was a raving lunatic. My "fireman/card playing/we'll go through hell with you, Pete, as long as you go first" friends must have thought I was nuts too when they saw my next move. I held out my hand and offered to shake his hand. I said "Hi, I'm Pete. How you doing tonight?"

First he stopped laughing, and then, to everyone's amazement, he shook my hand and said "I'm okay. I'm just having a little fun." He kept on feeling the texture of my latex-gloved hand, and this seemed to totally distract him.

I took this opportunity to sell him some needed life insurance by saying, "Why don't you have a seat in that car. You're looking kind of tired." I saw Barney remove his hand from the pistol grip. He did…sit in the car, I mean. I just made up that part about him looking tired, but it worked. The eight or so sheriffs and state boys couldn't believe what they were seeing. He walked over to a sheriff's car, opened the door, sat down, and then someone shut the door. They all looked at me, and I just remembered saying, "I'm history."

Back at the hall, the guys couldn't stop talking about how close I came to getting hurt, injured, disemboweled or scalped! As we resumed our card games, I said, "Anyone up to a game of Crazy Eights?"

Every Now & Then We Did Something Right

***

Don't get me wrong, my goal is not to make the volunteer firemen I worked with over the years, over the many years, over the many long years, sound like a group of bumbling idiots. Well, at least this night they weren't!

The whistle blew, and the response time was perfect. Eventually, everyone showed up. We had a real small crew together that night as everyone was under five-feet-ten-inches tall. Six of us in all. The stuffed toy Dalmatian sitting on the dashboard of the fire truck didn't count.

Our fire department had members from all different occupations. We had real heavy equipment operators, professional (usually over the road) semi truck drivers, not just one but a pair-a-medics, farmers who knew the lay of the land, an electrician with a shocking personality, and for extra measurement, a firewoman.

The call was a real house fire on a back, skinny, dirt road. The road had steep banks on both sides of it and was very hard to navigate. It would take skill (man) [I always wanted to write that] to drive the large pumper fire trucks to the location. This back, dirt road was iffy at best at holding these firetrucks' weight.

"I know of a field that is bone dry where we can get the trucks across to reach that house," one of the farmers said. We went to this field only to discover that a large tree had fallen across the entry culvert to the field.

"I'll go wake up Joe. He lives right over there. I'll borrow his bulldozer to move the tree," the real heavy equipment operator said. The tree was moved, and the trucks reached the house. The next obstacle was shutting off the electricity to the house (it was the cause of the fire).

"I'll do that!" the electrician said. Our paramedic was also a fireman and was on the scene for double duty if need be.

The firewoman did wonderfully at assisting to put out the fire by holding the hoses, spraying water at one end and serving hot coffee at the other end.

Considering the location of this house, the time of night and only having a skeleton crew show up, I felt we did a spectacular job at taming those flames and saving that house from burning to the ground. Sometimes things have a way of working out just right.

It's Never What You Expect

...

The previous stories that I've told you have had some excitement in them, but you must realize that not every call is "touch and go" or an extreme emergency. You really never know what to expect.

When I was working for an ambulance service many moons ago, I seem to recall a good many calls that were of the mundane nature. I'll give an example.

My partner and I were to transport an elderly man from a nursing home to a doctor's office. We did not know all the specifics of the office call, just that we needed to get him there and back to his nursing home in one piece. We transported him to the doc's office in what is called a wheelchair-compatible ambulance. You got it. The ambulance had a lift on the back to raise the wheelchair up so it could be pushed into the rig and secured with seatbelt-like straps. We did all of this, and upon arrival at the office, the nurse said it would just be a minute or two. This man was to receive an injection, and that was all. We waited a minute or two, and as promised, we were ready to make our return trip. We placed the patient, wheelchair and all, into the rig. Before we even got out of the driveway, this man slumped over in his wheelchair and was dead. Run it red, I yelled to my partner, and he did. The lights and siren were turned on, and we raced toward the hospital, which was about a thirty-second drive. During this thirty seconds, I earned two days pay. First, I noticed he wasn't breathing and had no pulse. Second, I knew I must start CPR on him.

Now is the time to explain something. Doing CPR on a dead person is a hard feat to master. Doing CPR on a dead patient in a moving ambulance is an even harder feat to conquer. Doing CPR on a dead guy in a moving wheelchair-compatible ambulance is just about impossible.

To do this feat, I had to get him out of that wheelchair. It was like moving d—(I won't say it) weight. Keep in mind that in this type of rig you have no gurney (ambulance bed) to place this poor soul on. So onto the floor of the rig he went. Real fast, I might add.

I began to perform CPR, and every time we went around a corner, he slid away from me and bumped into something inside the rig. It almost looked like a scene out of a Laurel and Hardy movie. If Red Skelton would have been riding shotgun, I'm sure he would have chuckled.

After what seemed like a millennium, we arrived at the hospital. I had been battered up a little, but the poor patient looked like he had been beaten up in a bar room brawl. I continued doing CPR until the good doctor told me to stop.

The cause of death was anaphylactic shock caused by an allergic reaction to the penicillin injection he had received at the doctor's office. You just never know what you're going to run into as an EMT.

1+1=3

Math has always been my weak subject!

▪▪▪

Three firemen go to a firemen's convention and agree to split the cost of the room (to save more money for needed refreshments).

The hotel manager informs them the cost of the room will be thirty dollars. They each give up ten dollars, and the bellboy carries their luggage up to the room. The hotel manager places a phone call to this room and says he made a mistake, that the cost of the room is only twenty-five dollars. The three firemen smiled, knowing they will have retained more slush money for needed fermented refreshments. The firemen take back one dollar each and give the bellboy the remaining two dollars for a tip.

Now, if initially the three fireman paid ten dollars each but were returned one dollar, that means each paid nine dollars. I know that three times nine is twenty-seven, plus the two-dollar tip the bellboy got would equal twenty-nine dollars. Then where did I lose the other dollar?

My dear, sweet wife Peggy, oh here she comes now, kissy-kissy-kiss, has a master's degree in mathematics, and on her final exam, she had this exact question minus the firemen on her test. It took her four pages to explain the procedure for answering this question correctly. Go ahead, give it a try.

[Some people will say I'm full of bull, but they are wrong…I don't even own a farm!]

Baby

...

Central dispatch came over the radio. "Rescue 123, you have a pregnant female [glad it wasn't a pregnant male] at the corner of 567 Pushing Place and 8910 Delivery Drive. You're out at 2400 hours, and have a nice trip!"

It has always astonished me that whenever you get what is known in the EMT world as "A Bad Call"—one that you would really like to let the other guys have—it always, always happens in a trailer. An EMT could go through his entire career and have a million halfway civil calls, and when the millionth and first call comes in as an emergency, it will be a pregnant, non-English-speaking alien with green skin, antennas and will be minutes away from delivering triplets! This patient will be located twenty-nine miles down a back dirt road. Three hundred yards off the road, he would find this patient while walking through a torrential downpour to be living *in a trailer*. I hate trailers!

When we arrived at the scene of this *trailer*, I mean pregnant female, I was told the contractions were about five or six minutes apart. With sweat dripping from my brow, I did some quick math and decided if we traveled at the speed of light, we should make it to the hospital just before she had this kid. But first we had to get her out of this *trailer*. Oh, did I forget to mention that she, along with the newborn baby to be, together weighed about 356 pounds? The baby was to weigh about six pounds, and I think you can do the math. Ever try to manipulate 356 pounds of weight that is lying on a seven-foot long wooden backboard with the guy lifting the other end of the backboard bearing a strong resemblance to Urkel around corners in a *trailer*?

So, here I am, en route to the hospital, talking on the radio to the hospital. "This is Rescue 123 to Hospital. We are en route to your facility with a thirty-seven-year-old pregnant *female* patient [Well, I couldn't let the dispatcher have all the fun.] who is presently in active labor." It had now been reported to me that this was to be this patient's sixth child. (She never told me that when we were at the *trailer*.) "Our ETA [estimated time of arrival] is ten minutes." I hung up the mike and asked my assistant (an EMT wannabe) to open up the obstetric kit just in case!

As if it could have turned out any other way, she was going to deliver, right there, right then, right now. "Stop the rig!" I said. There was about a thirty-second pause. "Rescue 123 to Hospital, we are en route to your facility now with two patients as of 0035 a.m. It's a girl!"

After grabbing the waving scalpel from the quivering hands of my assistant, I cut the already double clamped umbilical cord. I suctioned Sally Sue's mouth and nose out with a bulb syringe, then wrapped up this new present and let Mom take a good look at her.

After finally arriving at the hospital, the obstetrician said in a raspy, I'm-in-charge-of-the-entire-world voice, "Who delivered this baby?"

"I did," I said, thinking I may have done something wrong. This was only the second or third one I've ever done and considered myself a pro at it by no means.

"Here, you need to sign the Birth Certificate, as you delivered the baby," the obstetrician commanded.

"No problem, Doc," I said. I signed the paper, relieved in knowing that Mom and Sally Sue were left in good hands. I smiled, knowing that a new life had just begun.

Some fire departments will put different types of emblems on the outside of their ambulances to advertise their accomplishments. Ours had a four-inch-high stork holding a baby in a pink cloth blanket held in the stork's beak. I was given the honor of putting it on the ambulance, as it was I who delivered that baby in the ambulance. Once in an ambulance is enough!

I also delivered at least one baby in a house, one in an elevator and one in a car, but those will be stories kept for another day.

There's Danger Lurking Up Ahead

✦✦✦

The way I figured it out, which is probably incorrect, as math is still one of my weaker subjects, I could have gotten hurt or killed a zillion times while doing my Fireman/EMT thing. I believe that when it is your time, it will come no matter what you are doing at that given moment.

They say planes are safer to ride in than cars, percentage-wise, I mean. Don't believe 'em. Cars don't usually fall out of the sky!

Seeing how I am tangent-bound, I'll return to my main thought and speak of the dangers of being a Fireman/EMT.

Hepatitis is a disease that I'm told is one of the least pleasant ones to have. It can affect your liver and mess up your dance step for the rest of your life.

When I belonged to a fire department, they offered to any EMT or fireman, free of charge, the three Hepatitis shots. That way you would be protected and able to attend the next fireman's banquet to show off your new two-step moves.

I recommend that if you plan on getting involved, get the shots.

Lawsuits may make you a bit nervous, too. The bottom line with this issue is if you do things the way you were taught to do them, your worries are over. The Good Samaritan law will protect you. As stated, I have been EMTing for a while and have never been to court. Settling out of court is so much easier. *Smile*. Just kidding again. Put down that 1-800-LAWYER number!

The dangers of being a fireman is a separate book all its own. It would probably make the best seller list.

I will share this one story, as I want to clear my name as a coward.

I was at a house fire, and the chief wanted some men to put on Scott Air Packs and go inside this burning house to help put the fire out. Let me rephrase that. *The house was on fire*! I said, "Only a fool would put on that..." I put the pack on and entered the house. It gets about as hot in there as if you were standing inside of a house that was on fire. While in this house, my hose partner and I stepped back a few steps as not to disrupt the falling process of this wall that was trying its best to trap us in the front hallway. We backed on out of the house, and I told the chief right then and there, "Chief, unless there is some person inside a burning house that needs to come out, don't ever ask me to go inside of a burning house again. I do not like interior fire fighting.

To My Drivers

✦✦✦

I have often said, "Yep, I had to drive through twenty-nine feet of snow to reach the fire hall in a blizzard that was so cold it froze the very wind from blowing, snow just fell to the ground in lumps." My ambulance drivers also made that trip, and I don't want them to be forgotten. I have placed my life in their hands countless times, and I was always returned to the hall in one piece.

While encouraging a fellow (Is fellow right? This person's sexual origin is of the feminine nature) EMT during her initial training, I distinctly remember telling her that anything can happen out there at any time, and it did.

She and the driver were returning to the fire hall after going on a call when this happened.

Based in the southwestern New York area, we are accustomed to dealing with driving up and down large snow/ice covered hills. This is usually done without having an eighteen-wheeler coming up the hill at fifty miles per hour in your lane.

As the driver told the story, after his nerves were calmed, the semi slid into his lane and left nowhere for him to go except the ditch. The ditch was on a hill, and the ambulance, driver and EMT all went tumbling down a twenty-foot drop off. The ambulance rolled over three or four times. A few bumps and bruises occurred, and the light was broken off the top of the rig, but no one was seriously injured.

That never happed to me. The only things that ever happened to me were being shot at, an attempted stabbing, being spit on, yelled at, punched, slapped, bitten (human and animal), sworn at, threatened to be sued (but never was), rocks thrown at me, and a few more amenities I will leave out, none of which were by my drivers. Once again, I'll say thank you to you guys. You know who you are.

Mutual Aid

···

Mutual aid is when one fire department helps another fire department. This can be in the form of "Bring us a fire truck, Sparky," or "We may need more manpower, Shorty."

In my capacity, I would usually find myself assisting as an EMT

If more than one patient was to be transported, then there was a good chance that I would be riding in someone else's ambulance.

Just to paint a clearer picture, let me write that I've just arrived at the scene of a car accident. Four people are injured, and four ambulances are needed. A fellow EMT accompanied me to this gathering from our department. He "loads and goes" in our ambulance with eighteen-year-old, hourglass-figured Penelope Pitstop, who has a turned ankle. He leaves me stranded to care for the sixty-seven-year-old aggressive drunk, who is vulgar, dirty, has very bad breath, hasn't shaved in at least a week, and she is ornery. On top of all this, I get the pleasure of riding in another company's rig, where, by the way, I haven't the foggiest idea where they keep any of their equipment. I can't even find the tape.

Let's not forget the driver. In my own rig at least I know everyone that is allowed to drive this nicely-painted Winnebago with the red lights on top and loud siren to play with while he drives at high speeds, up hill and dale in all weather conditions! Another added option is the fact that the vehicle is top-heavy and usually sways quit nicely at top speeds.

I have ridden in an ambulance around a curve on two wheels before!

Now that I'm with another rig and driver, the game has changed. I don't know this guy or what he's done in the last twenty-four hours. For all I know, he could be Jack-the-Ripper's brother-in-law who has a distinct dislike for any medical personnel. Or maybe it's Captain Kangaroo's fourth cousin who has recently had his driver's license revoked!

The word that comes into play now is trust.

I'm just kidding, now. All you ambulance driver guys from southwestern New York put those shotguns back in the closets. I always was safe with you guys too, but how it frustrated me not being able to find that tape.

24/7

...

It didn't take me long to discover that being an EMT was a twenty-four hour a day, seven day a week commitment.

My wife Peggy and I bought Peggy's grandmother's house. We liked it, and we ended up living in it for nineteen years. Before we bought the house, we used to go out to Granny's on Sunday to have Sunday dinner. Man, could that woman cook. "How do you want your steak cooked, Peter?" Get the idea?

The country-cooked meal was ready. We had steak, mashed potatoes, peas, salad, and of course, homemade apple pie. After we sat down and started to eat, I noticed that grandma had an expression on her face that she had never shared with us before. When she acted as though she was trying to cough, the moment became serious. When her facial color turned a tinge of blue, I finally realized she was choking on a piece of steak. I had to react, and it had to be now, or this nice lady that cooked so well would die right in front of our eyes.

I should have said, "Peg, call 911," but I know I didn't. This was one of those many time-slowing-down moments that are so easily remembered and so hard to forget. I reacted as best as I could at that moment and quickly positioned myself behind Grandmother with my left knee on the floor as I crouched behind the chair that she was sitting in. I then placed my hands in the proper Heimlich Maneuver position. I thought right before I thrust my fist into her abdomen that I should sort of take it easy with her or I would break her bones. Then I remembered my instructor's voice saying, "If you want it to work, you need to be forceful." I was, and the lodged piece of steak came flying out. Then Granny said, "Peter, I couldn't breathe! If you hadn't squeezed me that way, I think I would have been a goner."

After drinking about eight cups of coffee to calm my nerves, I said, "Please pass the apple pie."

Our Neighbors

✒✒✒

We had nice neighbors when we lived at Granny's house. "Hi, Joan. Hi, Royal. How's the family? Royal, are you done with my socket set yet?"

Back in about '85 or so, Joan came running down to our house. "Peter, Joshua fell and broke his arm!" she said in a shaking voice. I ran up to Joan and Royal's house and saw Joshua sitting there with his broken arm.

"It's broken, alright," I said. I called 911. The ambulance came, and off to the hospital we went.

On another date: "Hi Peggy, is Peter home? Can he come up and take a look at one of the kids? I think…" I believe it was about this time that I remembered all of the free business my mom used to get when the word got out on her.

Friends

♥♥♥

"Rescue 123, your call is at such-and-such location with a complaint of a lawnmower accident. Central dispatch out at 1730 hours."

I heard this call come in over my home receiver and thought the address sounded familiar, but I couldn't put a finger on the residence until I got to the hall and someone said, "Isn't that the address of so-and-so's house? You know, the guy that belongs to our neighboring fire department?"

When I finally remembered whose address it was, I told the guys, "I know this guy pretty well.
Besides knowing him as a fireman, I also know him at my day job. We work together at the hospital." We arrived at the scene, and I had to keep telling myself to act as an EMT first and a friend and work associate second.

As I walked up to him, he said, "Oh no, not you!" He made this statement due to our working relationship, not to imply he wanted a different EMT. I don't think that is what he was implying, anyways. I told him we both needed to set work aside and deal with the present problem. The problem being that he had just cut off his right big toe with the lawnmower blade. I quickly assessed his amputation and stopped the bleeding by bandaging his foot tightly and elevating his right leg. The bleeding had stopped. I did look for the toe, but it was not to be found. It was pretty much mulched away on his front

110

lawn. The lesson I learned on this call was that accidents could happen to anyone at any time. If you live in a small rural area like I did, you will run into and care for friends and family. I decided that day to always be prepared for such a call. I re-supplied my first-aid kit that was still behind the front seat of my car.

The Parade

♪♪♪

Three years ago, our family moved out of the southwestern part of New York state and moved into the northwestern part of New York state; I thought my cousin was dumb! Actually, the weather has been much milder up by Rochester.

My kids Stefan and Susie were in seventh grade that year. Stefan plays the drums (like his dad Ringo…uh, um…Pete), and Susie plays the piano and the flute. They were playing in the Memorial Day Parade at a nearby town in their high school marching band. Susie, being of short stature, decided not to lug the piano down Main Street again, so she took and played her flute instead. Stefan had to carry the drum he played but not the whole set.

Yes, I'm one of those dads that have to camcorder every single breath that his children make. "Here they come," said Peggy. I got the tape rolling and got our fife and drum players immortalized on film. Actually, I plan on selling them all the footage I've taken over the years when they turn thirty or so. Hey—a guy's gotta have a backup plan for retirement nowadays.

The kids passed, and I put the camcorder away. Various departments from that area had their fire trucks and ambulances in the parade.

I happened to look to my right when I saw this middle-aged women fall face first to the sidewalk. I started to walk right toward her as my instincts kicked into action. I then noticed that one of the ambulances in the parade pulled right out of the parade and came over to her aid. At least he was on the ball.

It is surprising how most people act during an unusual situation. Most of the people kept watching the parade as if nothing had even happened. This lady's family was with her, of course, helping her, but I only saw one other person besides myself that was even concerned about the lady with the bleeding cut on her forehead.

I told the ambulance personnel that I wasn't in their department but would be glad to help. We dressed her wound, put on a neck collar and loaded her into the ambulance. Then they left.

As I stood there, seemingly alone in a crowd of thousands, I couldn't help but think of how times had changed. It's time for the general population to change how they feel and be willing to aid their fellow citizens.

The Cockatiel

...

"Let's go cherry picking today," I suggested to the family when we were looking for ideas to fill out our free Saturday afternoon.

"Okay!" said Susie in her five-year-old authoritarian voice. We—Peg and I—smiled at each other. We put Susie in her car seat, and off to the cherry orchard we drove.

On our return trip, I found myself thinking that I would try to attend the meeting at the fire hall that night. The county fire inspectors were to be there. It sounded like an interesting meeting, and Peg said I could go!

As we were returning from the cherry orchard, I rounded a curve about five miles from our village and stared in amazement to see thirty-foot flames shooting off of the roof of a house on a small hill to my left. I stopped the car on the side of the road and said to Peggy, "Drive to a phone and call 911 to report the fire," and then up the hill I ran.

Back in this period of time, cell phones weren't as popular as they are are now. As luck would have it, a man driving by stopped, had a cell phone and called 911. Peg and Susie sat in the car and watched as Susie munched on cherries.

After breathlessly reaching the top of the driveway, I saw a women in her mid-thirties and a boy I guessed to be about ten. I asked her if anyone was in the house, and she said no. At that moment, the boy broke away from his mother's grasp and ran into this burning house. I ran in right behind him, but he had the advantage of knowing the layout of his one-story house. I didn't! After searching for thirty smoke-filled seconds I found him struggling to free a birdcage from its holding stand. I released the cage, and he became cooperative to exiting his burning home. He, I, and the cockatiel came out the front door, all three of us coughing. Birds cough! I heard it.

I told this young man that he needed to stay by his mother's side to make sure she was kept safe. Okay, so I used a little reverse psychology. Just don't tell the psychiatrist I am working for about this story!

Off in the distance, I heard two different fire companies' fire whistles blowing. I began to circle the house looking for a garden hose, as if I was going to do much with it at this point. The house was now fully engulfed in flames. I also periodically looked back to make sure little Johnny was being the good Boy Scout that I told him to be. He was, so I went to the back of the house and saw a can of lawn mower gas sitting next to a wall that was smoking and burning. I grabbed the can to move it away from the burning wall when I heard fire trucks coming up the driveway. *Help at last*, I thought. I walked to the front of the house (still holding the gas can) and met our fire chief.

"Chief," I said, "I was the first one on the scene." As I began to tell him what I had first seen and done, I noticed he was laughing. I stopped talking, and he said, "Pete, turn around." Remember those fire inspectors I talked of earlier? All four of them were standing right behind me, looking at me holding that can of gas!

After the chief let them question me for a few minutes (just to make me sweat it out), he vouched for me. I was not an arsonist, and I was off the back burner.

It was probably five minutes later as I was asking Peg to go home and put the cherries away that one of my fireman buddies came up to me holding about ten boxes of shotgun shells.

"Pete, look what we found in that back room that was burning, right next to that wall where you moved that gas can."

"Let's put this thing out and go home," I said.

Peggy frowned at me; Susie continued to giggle.

I realized after that day that anything could happen at any time. Even something as strange as returning home and eating hot cherry pie.

Fireman

...

This book was originally supposed to be about me and my being an EMT. Boy, did you get led astray! I was also a fireman. As you can tell by the cockatiel story, I didn't really do too much EMT stuff at that call. This book would not be complete if I didn't share the other half of my voluntary experiences and the stories about my brothers, the firemen.

They placed their very lives in danger for me, and I for them.

After driving through eighteen feet of snow to reach the fire hall…oh, I already wrote that. We were called out to a car fire. How does a car catch on fire in the middle of the night in the middle of a blizzard, anyways? We took the pumper to this location, and yesiree-bob, there sat the car, and it was on fire.

Being four a.m., the turn out for this call hit the staggering number of three firemen. We pried up the hood where the fire was originating and started to put water to it. As I stood there holding the end of that hose, I thought, *Pete, what are you going to do if this car blows up?* By the end of that thought, the fire was out, and we went back home to bed.

Our department, at most, had only a scant number of medical personal. The fireboys would usually stay at home when they heard over their home receivers that the call was of a medical nature, but when it was anything else, they usually converged on that fire hall in droves. I did respond to the fire calls, but not as loyally as they did. I tried to do most of my living at my house and not at the fire hall. However, it was recorded that one year I responded to three hundred and fifty some calls. It was getting to be time that I had to slow down and let someone else pick up the slack...*the rookies.*

The Day the Sky Turned Black

As I awoke this morning, I could smell an odor that reminded me of a time when I was a youth. While growing up, I spent most of my adolescent (free time) years with my great uncle. His name was Sherman Skillman. To me, he was plain old Uncle Sherm. Back so many years ago, one of my favorite pastimes was spending time with him at what we called the sugarhouse. This was a building that was built in his woods where we cooked down maple sap in an evaporator and made maple syrup. I would trade my next ten paychecks to be able to relive just one of those spring days.

We used to get the fire really hot by burning car tires in this evaporator furnace-like structure. (It was almost legal to do that back then).

That was what I was smelling as I awoke. Burning tires.

The whistle blew and blew and just kept on blowing.

"Why isn't someone shutting that thing off?" I said to Peg as I ran out the front door to answer yet another call. *The sky was black*! The thought of Armageddon did cross my mind that morning. When I reached the fire hall, someone said, "The tire dump is on fire!" I checked to make sure I had my socks on, as I knew that this day would most likely turn out to be forty-eight hours long!

The aforementioned tire dump is in need of explanation. Have you ever seen fifty to sixty acres of land? Have you ever seen fifty to sixty acres of land covered with tires thirty to forty feet high? That was what we were dealing with.

Someone told me to take the rig, as it would probably be needed that day. When I left the hall with lights and siren going, I knew I wouldn't be home for dinner that night, probably not the next night either.

The tire dump was about two miles from the fire hall. When I arrived, I was directed to the triage area.

This fire was to have the largest turnout of any fire our county ever had, at least that I knew. There were fire trucks and heavy machinery such as bulldozers and backhoes that were coming in from all over the county. "The county disaster plan has been implemented," I heard one chief say to another.

No injuries yet, I thought to myself as I sat at the triage area. "I've got to see this fire up close," I said to my EMT partner. "I'm going to go up by the fire," I told him.

"Take a Scott Air Pack up with you," he suggested. "Some of those guys may need a whiff or two of oxygen." I put a Scott Air Pack on my shoulder. It's that oxygen tank and breathing mask you see firemen wear just before they charge into a burning building! Idiots!

I reached the top of the hill, which by the way was a quarter of a mile to a half-mile hike, wearing my rubber fireman boots, fireman's pants (called bunker pants), a fireman coat and that Scott Air Pack. Yes, I was sweating when I reached the top of that hill. It was hard believing what I knew I was really seeing. Acres and acres of tires of all kind were burning. If you have never seen a tire burn, read on.

The dump had every kind of tire imaginable, from the ordinary car tires to big eight- to ten-foot-wide equipment truck tires. When a tire is burning, it becomes extremely hot. I didn't have a heat meter (another made-up word. Boy, if my wife ever finds out about this…) on me, but I would guess they were burning at close to two thousand degrees Fahrenheit. I watched the fire travel towards the non-burning tires. When the fire came upon the non-burning tires, they almost exploded with flame. The fire just kept on refueling itself. The tires melted into liquid rubber as they burnt. The runoff was heading right down the hill towards a major county road. The boys down below with the backhoes were taking care of that situation.

Then something strange happened to me. I felt something move on my boots! I looked down towards my feet and saw between fifteen and twenty *snakes* tangling around my feet. I truthfully couldn't count them all as I was running at full speed while standing still. Being weighted down with one hundred pounds of accessories may have had a little bit to do with it, but the words phobia/paranoia also contributed to my motionless forward progress. It was like one of those nightmares we all have when you are moving quickly but not going anywhere. *I hate snakes*!

Snakes like tires, as they provide shelter and are a good place for them to catch bugs. Their homes got too hot, and they decided to come over and visit me. The boys at the top of the hill had a good laugh too!

I thought it was high time to return to the triage area, as I was sure they could not operate without me, so down the hill I ran. No one was in need of care when I arrived, so I borrowed some much-needed oxygen. "Man, Pete, is the fire that bad up there?" my partner asked me as I came running into the triage area, breathless.

"Never mind that right now; what are those two helicopters doing here?" I asked as we watched them circling around about three hundred feet up.

"Ah, I don't know," was his best answer.

We later found out that one helicopter held a news crew out of Buffalo, and the other held the county executive. He was assessing the situation from a bird's-eye view. I said to my partner, "I never was in Vietnam, but this sure looks like a scene out of one of their movies, doesn't it?" The choppers flew through the black wall of smoke and sent swirls towards the ground looking like little black tornados.

In the village where I lived, we had a fairly large elderly population. I took it upon myself to ensure that these elderly residents were informed of the fire and told to evacuate to relatives' homes in another town if possible. The air was putrid, and breathing was not easy for them.

Nighttime was upon us soon, and the fire kept burning. It was decided by the fire chiefs that the fire would be worked in shifts. We had no shortage of personnel, as most every department in the county was in attendance for this cookout. I took my turn squirting water (as I was intensely watching for any more snakes). We had a few medical calls, mostly smoke inhalation or fatigue, but nothing major.

The tire fire burnt for a long time and smoked for a longer time. That whole summer, a person could be reminded of the tire fire just by taking a sniff of the outdoor air.

My brother Tom (I can use his real name, and he won't sue me, as he still owes me twenty bucks from our last poker game at our last family reunion and would fear a counter suit.) lives in Charleston, South Carolina. He told me that he saw the tire fire on the National Weather Channel! "You might be wondering about this patch of darkness hovering over southwestern New York," the weather announcer said. He continued, "It's not a storm; it's a large tire fire."

In the Navy

My present thoughts are returning me back to my military days. I served for four years, and somehow or another I got shore duty for all four of those years. Popeye gone ashore!

I was an EMT at this time, also. I used to moonlight during my free time with a civilian ambulance service. I really didn't need the extra cash. I had plenty of gas in my new Camero; Uncle Sam was giving me "three hots and a cot," and I was able to safely get to Virginia Beach. I was realizing more and more that I was truly interested in this type of work.

Most sailors were on ships and were traveling the globe seeing far-off lands. Not me. My brother Phil was still stationed on a boat, home-ported in Hawaii, and the Navy frowned on having too many siblings floating at the same time. I was shore-duty bound and couldn't do a whole lot about it. I'm just glad the Army didn't find out!

I have told many people that my parents are the only parents in the southwestern New York area to have had four sons in the military at the same time. If I'm wrong, please let me know.

I worked this civilian ambulance service under a certificate known as a National Registered EMT Card. I'll tell you more about that later. Did I mention that they also have snakes in Virginia?

The call that I remember the most while EMTing in Virginia happened on a soggy August night. It was raining hard!

Our ambulance garage was located close to the city line of Portsmouth, Virginia. We took calls in the city and in the country.

We received the call; you guessed it, a 10-13. The location was out in the country, and it was terrain I was not extremely well versed on, so my partner drove. We ended up about twelve miles or so out in the sticks, and this event just kept on getting worse as it progressed.

My partner was a nice enough guy, but he was fifty-eight years old and didn't move too fast. He drove too fast, but when it came to actually moving on his own power, the tortoise lost the race every time.

We found the car in a ditch. It sat there after turning over several times and finally coming to rest. I was leaning into the car and caring for the semi-conscious driver when I heard The fire chief tell my partner, "I heard the call on my scanner and came to help. I know this car. I don't know the driver, but this car was in my driveway three days ago. I believe it belongs to a friend of my son."

I was wearing fireman boots, so I volunteered to take a flashlight and search the area in the brush for anyone else. The driver was answering questions, but he was giving the wrong answers—i.e. unreliable—he was not Richard Petty, even if he said he was. The boots, you may be wondering? Would you be walking around in the bushes in the dark in Virginia *where they have poisionous snakes* without boots on? I didn't think so!

I searched until my partner had the driver almost ready to go. I came back to the road just as the wrecker was pulling the car out of the ditch, and we put the driver into our rig. The car moved in a funny motion as if it was rolling over something as the wrecker pulled on it. It was—the helpful chief's son.

Needless to say, the chief went totally berserk. My partner heard the policeman on the scene call a coroner and for another ambulance to care for the chief. I was glad when that night ended.

Helicopters, Jets and Planes

✦✦✦

When I was a corpsman (pronounced core-man) in the US Navy, I had a very unique job.

When I arrived at Portsmouth, Virginia, I was given four choices of places to work as a corpsman. I chose working in the largest newborn nursery and Nursery Intensive Care Unit on the east coast. If not the largest, it pulled in a close second place. This place was cool. Together, both units housed more than one hundred babies most of the time. We got a new batch about every three days. I volunteered for this job, as I didn't like the other choices. I chose working with the kids, as the other selections didn't have that Skillman appeal. I didn't want to get stuck working on an orthopedic floor, where they convert you into professional weight lifters, and I didn't have the heart to work in the cardiac care unit! The morgue was a dead end, so for now anyways, it was going to be me, those babies and Pampers.

The kids all belonged to either military dependant wives—i.e. the lady's husband was a grunt, G.I., flyboy, or an anchor clanker. There were also cases when Mom was active duty personnel herself. If this was the case, Mom was expected to return to active duty shortly after receiving her new arrival. If the baby had a medical problem and needed more shore leave to recuperate, then they stayed with us until we made sure they were ship shape.

When the infant was healthy and it was time to ship out, the Lt. Docs gave the young recruit his traveling orders, and that's when I came into the picture.

The military frowned on sending infants traveling around the countryside alone, so they supplied them with an escort...*me*.

I would volunteer for this job every chance I got as it gave me travel, hazard duty pay (when I flew, and that was most of the time) and a patient that didn't send in complaints to the admiral about care received. I got to eat his peanuts on the plane too!

I was able to fly from Virginia to various places in the US during this (Return the Baby to Mom) program. The military's policy was to get the kid back to Mom as fast as possible, and the corpsman could hitchhike back to base. I didn't really have to hitchhike back, but it wasn't far from it. I learned just about every back road in the south as I made most of my return trips to Portsmouth, Virginia, on a bus.

I recall reporting to the airport with an infant one day. We arrived in a military ambulance, and the crew loaded the infant inside what was called an Isollete. It was a desk-sized, plexiglass-looking box that held the baby securely. We didn't want any AWOL's to occur while in flight. The pilot told me to sit in the seat next to the Isollete, and seeing how he was an officer and I wasn't, I scrambled to the seat. I said, "Sir, I can't see the baby if I sit down, as the Isollete is too high."

"Well, I'll fix that, sailor!" the captain of the plane said. He told me to stand up, and he proceeded to put one of those wide green military belts around my waist. Then he snapped four connecting straps to the belt and secured them to various snap holding places around this plane. I forgot to mention that this plane was a Phantom Jet. I rode, standing up, at about six-hundred miles per hour from Virginia to Texas in record time. Talk about surfing the net. I surfed across half the nation that day standing up in that plane while monitoring little Sailor Sam.

I delivered Sammy to his destination, and I was lucky that my orders said to return to Virginia by plane and not by bus that time. That was the usual case when I would fly to Camp Lejeune, North Carolina. I got so I knew every pothole from there to Norfolk, VA.

My ride back to Virginia was in the largest medical plane the US Air Force owned at the time. Have you ever been on a plane and heard someone say,

"Is there a doctor on board?" If that question had been asked on this ride, half the crew of about one hundred would have stood up. It was like riding in a three-story hospital in the sky. I only got lost once!

I mention this and other military stories to show more of the foundation that was laid prior to me doing EMT stuff. The things I learned in the military helped me immensely, as I was prepared to answer the call.

The Infants

▝▝▝

No man or woman
Stands as tall
As the one that stoops
To raise the small

One of the neatest things we corpsman, corpswaves, nurses and doctors did at the NICU in Virginia was to save the life of the second smallest baby in the world in 1977. She weighed in at a whopping fifteen ounces! Tammy, we all still love you.

The sad memories that I still carry are that we didn't save them all.

I dedicate this story to all the infants that passed away in the Nursery Intensive Care Unit in Portsmouth, Virginia, where I served as a United States Navy Senior Corpsman for three and a half years.

I used to work what was called a rotating shift. After all was said and done, the only thing that ended up rotated was me.

Within a month's time, I would work at least one week of first, second and third shift. Now do you see why I volunteered for escort duty? (It kept me on the first shift longer.)

I was pulling a week of third shift when all this happened, but first let me explain a few details.

As stated, the ward I worked on was the Newborn Nursery and the Nursery ICU. The Newborn Nursery was the training ground for corpsman who wanted to work in the NICU. First they had to prove they could feed and change a baby without dropping it (before we would allow them to get to the more technical stuff). We did have some that didn't make the cut.

While being in the position of the Senior Corpsman of the Newborn Nursery I was in charge of about twenty-five other corpsman. This one corpsman, whom I won't call by name just yet, was a civilian at one time. I believe his occupation then was being a Kentucky squirrel hunter. This guy was beyond dumb. When I saw that movie *Dumb and Dumber*, I thought of him. I also thought of him the day that Naval Intelligence Service visited me and Hospital Corpsman Pile after he discharged the wrong baby to the wrong mother. Knowing that intelligence is hereditary, I guessed that the wrongly discharged baby's mother may have been kin to him, but I don't have proof of that.

Needless to say, he didn't make the team of the NICU Corpsman, and I did. There were many days when I had wished that I didn't make that team.

The NICU (Nursery Intensive Care Unit) had an average of ten to fifteen infants that were in critical status, at best. Most were on ventilators that were called Baby Bird Ventilators. These assisted the baby with breathing.

It would be an almost everyday occurrence for one of these kids to go into cardiac arrest. The corpsmen were the ones that did the deed of CPR.

As I was saying, I was pulling third shift. Working that night in the NICU was an experienced RN, me and an inexperienced RN who had just graduated from RN school. She was known as Ensign Bensign, i.e. Brainless! The lieutenant was taking a break when the filled diaper hit the fan.

One of the kids I was assigned to coded—i.e. went into cardiac arrest. I calmly disconnected the ventilator from the kid and grabbed the infant-sized AMBU-Bag. As I was doing CPR on junior, I asked Ensign Bensign to please call a doctor. I heard no movement behind me. I turned and saw her frozen in place like a popsicle on a stick. She was in shock, and I was on my own.

Miss Bensign had never seen CPR done on an infant before and was not holding up too well at that moment.

Then the unheard of happened. A child that was assigned to the Lt. Nurse coded. I felt I had nothing to loose at this point except for two lives, so I leaned over and unplugged the warmer that Baby #2 was lying on and pulled it close to me. I started to perform CPR on two babies at the same time. Don't try this at home! I started to yell to attract attention but got none. Little Miss Lowest-on-the-Officer-Ladder still wasn't moving. Her eyes were wide open as she stood stiffly. No signs of melting were present!

Finally, an E-2 corpsman who had been outdoors came walking by an open window. "Get in here!" I yelled to him. He did, as he must have thought I was an officer—I was wearing hospital scrubs, as all NICU personnel did. He telephoned and was able to get me a few doctors.

When the docs showed up I collapsed into a chair after doing this dual CPR trick for about eight or nine minutes.

To end this story on a positive note, I will state that both babies lived, and so did I. For me, it was a close one. I was at the tender age of nineteen when this all happened, and when I went back to the barracks the following morning, I felt as if I was pushing fifty.

I was presented with a Letter of Commendation from a two-star admiral for this and other tricks of the trade I performed at the NICU in Portsmouth, Virginia.

When I got out of the Navy and started to work at a civilian ambulance service, I was told that my National Registered EMT Card that I used while in the Navy was not accepted in New York state, the reason being that I only scored seventy-four percent on the national test, and in NY, you needed to have a seventy-five percent or higher.

I knew I should have gotten that Gold Master Card when I had the chance! Sorry, I was just having a bad brain moment.

I was told I must have a New York state EMT card to allow me to work on this newly acquired ambulance job I found in southwestern New York state.

To burn up a lot of spare time I had while in the Navy, I took a bunch of military courses while I was in the Non-Floaters Portsmouth Boat Club. I took Infant Cardiac Care, the Dos and Don'ts of Brain Surgery and Ambulance Driving 101...crash...I resubmitted my application for the NY State EMT card accompanied with about twenty of these military diplomas.

I got in the mail a few weeks later my New York state EMT card, along with a letter that stated as follows:

> Dear Sir:
>
> You will find your EMT card for New York State enclosed.
> Know that you are the only person to date to obtain this card with a score of under seventy-five percent.
> Have a nice day.
>
> > Signed:
> > So-and-So Big Wig,
> > Albany, New York 147??

Now, who says you can't bridge the gap?

The Missing Girl

***

Pagers are a wonderful thing. For example, when you and your buddy are heading off to the pizza and chicken wing place to get some pizza and chicken wings for your poker-playing buddies back at the fire hall, the pager has the ability to call you back to the hall before you even get halfway down to the pizza and chicken wing place.

Over the pager, we heard that a neighboring company was looking for a missing girl at an area lake. In other words, a possible drowning.

"Let's head over," I said. "I'm losing at the hall anyways."

My buddy happened to be the chief of our company, so he hit his red light, and we raced off to help with the effort to find this girl.

On our arrival, we couldn't believe how many boats were out on this little half-mile long by quarter-mile wide lake. "It looks like about fifty boats out there," he said.

"Yep," I replied. We walked toward the lake and saw a small seaworthy rowboat that had been pulled halfway out of the water. It needed a paint job, but besides that, it looked pretty good. "Wonder why no one is using this one?" I asked.

"We might as well," the chief said. We were about to board this vessel but were momentarily distracted as we both looked down and saw the missing teenage girl, highly intoxicated and lying motionless, except for her breathing, in the bottom of this rowboat. "She's over here!" we both yelled at the same time to the people out on the lake.

The next scene resembled that of a James Bond movie. You know, the scene when all of the boats come at you all at once and make you feel like you want to be somewhere else!

She was breathing just fine, but man was she crocked. We turned care over to their EMT. In the fireman's world, it's politically correct, and we headed for home.

"Hey chief," I said, "I'm getting pretty hungry! Do me a favor and turn that pager off for a while, will ya?"

Bingo

❝❝❝

A book is not anywhere near done unless you mention Bingo. (It's not anywhere near done anyways, so keep reading.)

Wednesday night bingo. How could I almost forget? Most fire departments have bingo as one of their primary incomes. The firemen and EMTs are all voluntary. So is the help at Wednesday night bingo. If my memory serves me right, I can remember countless bingo nights when we ran the show with a skeleton crew. The job got done, and we had a lot of fun doing it, but we sure could have used a little more help.

I introduced my two oldest kids (Stefan and Susie) to bingo. I believe that, the way the law reads, if they are under eighteen years old, then they have to be accompanied by an adult. That's where Grandma Bingo comes into the picture. My friend and main ambulance driver, we'll call him Sleepy, as I was Doc. He wasn't Grumpy or Sneezy or any of those other short guys. Dopey maybe, but that's another chapter. So we'll call him Sleepy, as that was the state of mind he was usually in, except, of course, not when he was driving the ambulance.

Sleepy always brought his mother to bingo. She adored Susie and Stefan and took them under her wing, so to speak. She showed them how to fly at playing bingo. I usually worked the floor or assisted the number caller and felt relieved knowing that Susie and Stefan were sitting next to the bingo champ!

Over the years, my kids never won at bingo, but I'm sure they will never forget Grandma Bingo and all the fun they had with her.

In a small, close-knit village like that one, it just came natural for relationships like that to develop. At the time, my wife's mother had passed away, and so did mine. This left the kids with no grandmother. The gap was filled. If you're reading this, Grandma Bingo, thank you.

The fire hall had many events to reinforce unity with its members and the community. The turkey raffles were presented every year, and Halloween parties were held for the kids. (We figured if we kept them occupied inside, they wouldn't be getting into trouble outside). Other various year-round gatherings were held to make the fire hall a place where you wanted to be. *Bingo*!

DOA

***

As a youth, I spent a considerable amount of time with my Great Uncle Sherm, as previously mentioned. All of my memories of him are dear to me, except one!

One bright, sunny summer morning, my Uncle Sherm and I were up in his woods cutting firewood for his use at home. I loved riding in that wagon full of cut firewood. We traveled towards the end of the woods while I was being bumped and jostled. *This is better than any amusement park ride!* I thought. "Pete, would you come down after lunch and help me unload the wood from the wagon?" my great uncle asked.

"Sure will," I replied. Except for my father, this man drew more respect from me than any man walking. Short of breaking the Ten Commandments, I couldn't think of much I wouldn't do for him. All he had to do was ask.

My Great Uncle Sherm went to his home and ate lunch. I did the same at mine. I walked down the road about one half mile to his house after lunch and found him lying dead on the ground next to the tractor. Uncle Sherm had died from a massive heart attack. At fifteen years of age, I only knew that he was dead, and I didn't like it. I was in shock, but I was also unaware of that at the time. I thought, "I need to tell someone." I walked into his house and saw my Great Aunt Belle washing dishes at the sink and listening to her favorite religious radio station. *She couldn't know*, I surmised. I needed to reach deep down inside myself and find enough maturity to enable me to tell my great aunt that her husband had just passed away not thirty feet from her. I broke the news to her as gently as I knew how. In my mind alone, I became a man that sunny summer afternoon.

10-13

...

"Rescue 123, your ambulance is requested by the large oak tree on the old country road for a 10-13. Central out at 1300." For those that may have forgotten the Police/Fireman 10 codes, a 10-13 refers to a car accident. Those two numbers had a way of putting a chill down your spine!

Going to the scene of a car accident tends to create a feeling in an EMT unlike any other call. While en route to a scene labeled 10-13, your mind tends to paint all the pictures of all the previous car accidents that you have been to. They usually turn out worse than you've anticipated.

We had to drive fifteen miles. Even at top speeds, I had plenty of time to re-run many thoughts through my mind. From the back of the rig, I watched through the windshield as we approached the scene. *Why is it that everyone is just standing next to this car accident when they should at least be trying to do something?* I was thinking as my adrenaline was pumping at top speed. I exited the rig. This four-and-a-half-foot car used to be full sized. Parts of the car lay over one hundred feet away down the road, in the field, and in the stream that ran slowly by the roadside. They had flown off of the car. I will not describe in detail what I saw when I looked into the car out of respect for the dead. He was pinned in the car and was unquestionably very dead. The policeman told us that for this much damage to have occurred, the pinned driver must have been traveling in excess of one hundred miles per hour when he hit the middle of that old oak tree. It took over an hour to extricate him from the car. No one seemed to be in a hurry. Suicide or accident, we never knew.

In CPR class, they teach the EMT that cardio-pulmonary resuscitation should be started with an absent pulse unless death is apparent. This can be seen by rigor mortis (an extreme stiffening of the body) or by the viewing of a lividity line. When the body dies, the blood, of course, is still, and it will settle in the body. The discolored area where the blood has settled is darker than the areas where the blood has drained. The separation of these two different areas is known as the lividity line.

As an EMT, I only had two DOAs. The other was an elderly woman that lived alone. The family had not heard from her for a few days, so they called the police to investigate. They called us! We found her in her bed. Our guess was that she had passed away two or three days prior. We were wrong. The coroner said two weeks!

Violent Patients—Violent Families

▪ ▪ ▪

When an ambulance is called, it's a safe bet that something is wrong somewhere. Usually when something is wrong, people get anxious, upset and may act on different impulses than what is usual for them. That's when violence occurs.

What's Wrong with My Dad?

♪♪♪

Upon our arrival, I found a middle-aged man who was having difficulty breathing; his skin color was cyanotic (very light blue in color), and he was very anxious. I knew from a visual assessment that this person was in trouble (medical trouble), and I called for a paramedic.

One of the luxuries of being an EMT is that whenever you got into something that was too deep, and you were in way over your head, you could always call for a paramedic to bail you out. The feeling reminded me of the feeling I often felt when Mom was in that first-aid class with me.

The paramedic said he could be at our location in seven to ten minutes. After doing my initial assessment and hearing this man's heart beat over 160 times a minute, I was sure he was in trouble. It was most likely a heart condition known as v-tach or ventricular tachycardia. Then his lights went out. He was unresponsive to my voice or to touch. *Where is that paramedic?* I thought. This person needed to be cardioverted (to have his heart shocked to allow it to stop for a moment and hopefully start back beating up again at a slower pace.) At the time, basic EMTs were not allowed to do this procedure. I had administered oxygen by mask to him, but that wasn't enough. His heart stopped all at once, and it was up to me to try to save his life!

That was the moment of truth; that was what I've been trained for.

Then, like a chill from the night, I heard a voice say, "What's wrong with my dad?" a young boy of nine or ten shrilled. One of the firemen distracted him by giving him his best reasonable explanation. It worked, and the boy was out of my hair for the moment. I needed to start CPR, and I was the only one there that knew how. With pulse and respiration absent, I tore open his shirt to find the correct spot for placing my hands. I gave two breaths of air by way of the AMBU-Bag. I then started to compress his chest downwards with my hands. The ten-year-old boy was not being distracted well enough, came running towards me and started to hit me on the back, screaming, "Don't do that to my daddy!" Doing CPR by yourself is no fun. It's a lot less fun having a boy beating on you while you are doing it!

"Someone get him," I said. I tried not to lose my rhythm, and then I saw the paramedic walk in. He did his thing, said clear and delivered the shock. He shocked him twice, and we had a pulse. "Load and go!" he said, and we did.

This story did have a happy ending. I found out later he survived and was returned home in about a week.

The boy did not know why I was pushing down on his dad and acted out of frustration and his form of violence.

♪♪♪

Two EMTs were sitting in their ambulance at a red light. The radio was turned on, and they started to hum to the song playing. At the same time, a large truck ran right through the red light. "Was that an International or a Mack?" the one EMT asked the other.

"Neither," was the reply from the other EMT while listening intently to the radio. "That was a Fleetwood Mac!"

Now do you see why I still have two jobs!

That's My Wife

***

I remember a call we got one cold October night while I was working in a nearby city. A lady in her fifties had fallen on some outdoor steps and was unresponsive when approached by a police officer. We were called to this scene, and as I was doing my initial assessment, a man…a big man…a very big man came running up the sidewalk, yelling, "That's my wife; get away from her!" The large man was pretty much in the same boat as the ten year old from the last story, the main difference being he was drunk.

I was thankful the officer was still there to encourage that man not to do me bodily harm. I'm frail, you know! The only problems the lady had to deal with were a bump on her head and her drunken husband when she rejoined the conscious world.

Drugs

👃👃👃

I was called to a home that was…let's say…remote! I got off the dogsled (just kidding) and entered the house. The sheriffs (three of them) were there before us and warned us, "This guy could be trouble!"

When I walked into his living room, I saw him. He was sitting in his recliner with his left wrist bleeding profusely. "Hi, what's happening?" I said to him as I noticed his tie-dyed t-shirt.

"Get the -ell away from me, or I'll cut you next!" I could tell this was not going to be a pleasant social visit.

When threatened, the experienced EMT has two choices: 1) run, or 2) run faster! At this point, the police took over and informed this gentleman (I use that term loosely) that if he didn't allow us to treat his serious injury, then he would be placed under arrest. Did you know that it is against the law to attempt suicide?

Why, what is this world coming to?

The Woodstock alumnus got up out of his chair and held out a butcher knife that was two feet long if it was a mile. He was going to take on the whole force. I do remember seeing at least one gun drawn not three feet away from me, so I took to running seriously at that moment! The police subdued him, and after they retrieved me from afar, I was told I could now treat him.

Treating someone with a cut wrist who is wearing handcuffs is a challenge. I did what I could to stop the bleeding. The nice man and two of our county's finest sheriffs rode to the hospital with me in the back of the ambulance.

Information that came to me later (from a very reliable source—the EMT gossip room at the hospital) informed me that Woody had taken his alphabet literally that day. L, S, and D were his letters of choice.

Humor Is a Wonderful Thing!

I wish I knew some

***

I suppose that I could write a few chapters about the *fat lady* that got stuck in the bathroom stall or about the guy that got part of his male anatomy stuck in a place where it shouldn't have been in the first place, but I won't bore you with those details, as everyone has already heard them a million times anyway.

The story I would like to share is one that I didn't witness when it happened but heard about many years later. This story survived the test of time. That's how you can tell if it's a good one!

The Man That Stuttttered

...

As in many fire halls, men (and women too, at least at our department) have been known to sit around the hall on cold winter nights during a blizzard and pass the time by telling stories. They sit, wait, hope and pray that the whistle doesn't blow.

"Pass me that thar coffee pot, will ya, Pete? Hey, did I ever tell you about the time in *unnamed town* [don't want this guy to come after me with a pitchfork] that they had a huge fur [translated as fire], and it took them all day to put it out? No? Well, it was a big one, and it took them all day. And I'm tellin' you now…" Snorrre. "They tell me it happened way back in forty-one. It was just about the time we got these new-fangled furman radios that allowed us to talk to one tuther. Are you awake, Pete?"

"Yah."

"Well, anyways, thar was this here furman named Leroy, and when he talked, he stuttered. You know, kind of like a Thompson sub-machine gun! Anyhow, all these furman had a been battlin' this blazin' fur all day long and were in need of a little something to brightin' up thar day. Why, by gum, they got it!"

Now the way this old timer told it to me, "These here men was a-puttin' away all the fur equipment, and everyone wanted to get thar turn on talkin' on them new fur radios."

Leroy did too. Various non-critical messages were heard over them there fur radios, like, "BR549, we got to bring all those hoses inside before they get wet!"

"Roger, 10-4"

"This ain't Roger, this here is Henry!"

And then they would hear, "Hey Tom, hurry up and get over into the truck so we can go back to the hall were it's nice 'n warm. It's cold out here, and it's startin' to rain like hail!"

Ol' Leroy thought it was about time to give it a whirl, and he decided to call the main county headquarters up at the county seat. Then he goes and says, "Count, count, county sssseat. This here is ba, baba, ba, base BR fa-fa five four nine and wa, wa, wA, *we* got all the eee, equip, equipa, equipment ba, baba, ba, back into the fire fa firehall na, na, now. BR5 fo-fo four nine ow, ow, out."

Dead radio silence happened for the next thirty seconds over the entire county. Then, the county headquarters came back and said, "Okay, Leroy, you're clear at 2200 hours." Thirty more seconds passed by. Then we all heard Leroy say, "Ba, ba, BR five four na, na, nine to count, count, county seat. Ha, ha, ha, how di, di, didja know it was ma, ma, me?"

After hearing this story, a few things became clear to me. First, volunteer fire departments were, and still are, manned by everyday, ordinary people that are good-hearted and sincere. Second, nobody is perfect, and nobody will ever let you forget it, either.

❊ ❊ ❊

A nice gentleman died and went to heaven. Upon his arrival, he said to the gatekeeper, "I sort of figured I would end up here, but is it possible for me to see the other place just for curiosity's sake?"

"Sure can, bub. Just get on that elevator and push the H button," the gatekeeper instructed.

The man got in, pushed the button and descended for a long time. When the elevator door opened, the man looked out the door in amazement. He was first hit with a blast of cold air as he noticed huge icicles hanging everywhere. The temperature was freezing. The devil walked up to him and said, "I'll bet you weren't expecting this, were you?"

"No!" the gentleman replied.

Then the devil said, "This all happened when some guy named Pete Skillman finally drove a fire truck without running it into anything!"

Okay, so I had to fill up a page. Give me a break, will ya!

We All Gotta Have Our Fun—The Rookie

...

Walking into any fire department and asking to join the sorority is a dangerous endeavor for anyone to undertake. Life and limb are at stake. Mostly life.

Billy (fake name) was a nice kid. He just turned eighteen and felt compelled to be behind the wheel of that big, new, shiny red fire truck. It wasn't that his lifelong dream was to be a Johnny Gage wannabe, he just wanted to show off to his new girlfriend his newly-acquired driving skills and hadn't accumulated the funding yet to purchase his own vehicle.

We used to love the rookies. It gave us the opportunity to share our vast knowledge of fire fighting, our understanding of the mechanical application of all the fire equipment. Most importantly, it gave us the chance to pay someone back for all the mean tricks that were played on us when we were green behind the ears.

It went something like this: "Okay, Billy, the first thing you need to learn is that, with fire hoses, we have a variety of different sizes. Now you see, this hose here has an outside circumference of a quarter of an inch, and this one is a half an inch round. Are ya with me so far, Billy? Now the really big hose on the top of the truck is the largest one we carry. No, it wasn't a joke, Billy, so stop laughing. It's the granddaddy of them all, and it's a three incher." The

Chief said at the meeting just last night, "Yes, Billy, I know you weren't there at the meeting last night." He said, "The *department* needs to add more three-inch hose onto that truck today, but as of right now, we can't afford to go out and buy new hose, so we'll have to do what we've always done." *Pause.*

"What's that Pete?" Billy asked blankly.

"Oh never mind for right now. We're not supposed to go running around the county with these trucks looking for stuff. For these trucks to roll, there has to be an emergency, and I can't go and get it as my car is in the garage being fixed."

"Pete, what is it that we need? I got a bike."

As he nibbles at the hook, "Billy, does it have a basket on it?"

"*Yes!*"

"Well maybe you could fit it in there."

"What is it? Where do I go?" As he bites, I reel him in!

"Well, Bill, if you really want to help out the *department*, you could ride your bicycle down to our neighboring fire department (fourteen miles down the road) and ask them if we could borrow their hose stretchers for a day or two. Whatever you do, William, don't forget to tell them we'll bring them back as soon as we are done with them. The last guy that had them, well, we'll never hear the end of that one. By the way, do you have your brand new fireman's card on you? They might want to 'proof' you to see if you're the real deal."

"Sure do, Pete! Got it in the mail just this morning," Billy echoed.

"Okay, then. We're all set." I informed him. "So I'll see you in what, about three or four hours?" "Okay, bye ,Pete," He said.

"Goodbye Billy."

Later, down at the neighboring fire department…

"So you say *Pete Skillman* sent you down here for those hose stretchers, huh. Well, I remember when he walked all the way down here from his department back in '84 asking for the same thing. Oh yah, when you see Pete again, ask him if he ever found that bucket of steam to wash the trucks with and that left handed screwdriver, will ya!"

And I Remember When

...

After a night at the hall, having volunteered to work bingo, that cold blizzard Wednesday night, the boys and I decided to retire upstairs to the game room and get down to some serious reminiscing before braving the elements on our journey home.

Since there was some serious snow falling outside, the topic of discussion seemed to be generated by the present weather conditions. I sat there patiently and listened to various tales of how back in '38 or '39 (an old guy was telling this one) it got so cold outside that all ice fishing in the county was cancelled. It seems the fisherman couldn't drill far enough through the ice to reach the water. (I didn't believe that one either).

Then someone told the one about snowplowing through drifts that were almost as high as the telephone wires.

Ted told one about how his entire family of thirteen was snowed in up in the hills for two months. To survive they had to eat their pets and then were forced to eat the reindeer as they landed on the roof. Now that one I believed!

I finally got my turn to address the countless masses (five) and told the story of how my brother Phil and I used to make snow tunnels at our home. We were only about seven or eight. I said, "I don't know if it was because I was shorter then or if the snow was deeper back then, but I do remember we used to spend hours burrowing through the snow to make a maze of snow tunnels. I recall one day we lost our direction after starting the tunnel from the front door of the house. Our plan of attack was to tunnel over to the garage so we could have a secret passageway from one building to the other." I looked over at Mr. Wilson, who seemed to be taking an interest in my story. "My older brother Phillip and I pushed away the last of the resisting snow and found that we had tunneled ourselves out to the road. I had to yell, 'Quick! Back into the tunnel!' It was a good thing that he listened to me, for we no sooner got five feet back into that tunnel when a county snow plow swooshed by and took out the end of our tunnel."

"And do you remember that plow driver walking up to your house and talking to your mother about you kids being next to the road?" Mr. Wilson asked.

"Yes, I do. How did you know that?" I asked.

"I was driving that snowplow that day," he scolded again.

"Now it's my turn to tell one," Wilson said. "Back in the winter of '42...no, Bob, not the summer of '42."

"That was a movie," I corrected.

Mr. Wilson continued to say, "I and about ten other firemen were downstairs when all of a sudden we heard a voice coming over the radio in the radio room." It said, 'This is truck 15, and I'm stuck up on route 101 by the relay station. I can't get my plow truck out of this drift, and if I don't get some help soon, I will freeze to death!' You could have heard a pin drop, that is, if anyone was sewing at the time, which none of us men were. We just sort of looked at each other," he said. Then someone said, 'Where the heck is that guy? There's no route 101 in this county, or in this state as far as I know,'" Wilson continued. "So I walked over and pressed the mic on the radio and started to talk to the guy. I said, 'Who's calling, and what is your exact location?' He said his name was Allen something or another and that he was stranded in a huge snowdrift on top of a mountain on route 101 in the state of Washington. Now for you boys that have forgotten, we are in the state of New York. This Allen fellow also said that he had been trying to radio someone for over three hours with no answer, that his truck was running out of fuel and that he wouldn't be able to walk to the nearest house, twenty miles away. That boy was in some serious trouble. We asked him for his base's phone number and told him we would call them. We told him who we were, and right after he gave us the numbers, the radio connection faded out."

Wilson said it was about two hours later when the department received a phone call from somewhere in Washington State. It was from the highway department's base where this Allen fellow worked. They said they found him and that he was okay. We figured that the weather conditions that day were causing his message to travel across the United States, bouncing off of clouds or what is known as radio skip. "That guy's life was saved because of bad weather!" Wilson ended.

I believed that story too!

You Have to Keep a Level Head as an EMT

...

I sure hate to sound redundant, but it really was the middle of winter, in the middle of the night, in the middle of a blizzard, and I was in the middle of a really, really good dream when that fire whistle went off and went off and went off.

Being smarter than the average bear, Boo Boo, I took extra time and made sure that my winter coat was securely on prior to rushing out the front door, through the bitter cold, over the snow bank to my half buried car, without any socks on to answer yet another call.

At the time, I only lived about a mile from the fire hall, but it was not to be my destiny to reach the hall that night. I rounded the curve to the right, and there it was, another car accident.

This accident occurred between my house and the fire hall. I heard the ambulance coming, so I stopped to see what I could do prior to its arrival. A small pickup truck had hit a small car, and it didn't look too bad. I assessed the man driving the truck, and he looked to be without any injury. The ambulance stopped, and a fireman came over to me. I told him to keep an eye on the guy, as I needed to assess the person in the small car. As I approached this small car, I saw that the impact had shattered the rear window. The lady (we'll say fifty to be polite) was seat-belted in the driver's seat and was rambling on, saying, "Where is she? Where is she?"

I asked her, "Who are you referring to?"

"Why, my sister, of course," she said. I looked at the others standing around and noticed another EMT.

I said to him, "Can you get her vital signs? I'm going to take a look around and find her sister."

The car and truck had not traveled far from the road after the impact, and at best, I could only see three or four hundred dollars worth of damage to both vehicles. I kept thinking about that rear window being smashed and wondered if someone could have been ejected from the rear of the car. I got a flashlight and started looking. The storm had let up some, and visibility was improving. I shone the light out over the fields and saw no one. I was returning to the car when I noticed a snowdrift I hadn't checked, so I shined the light towards it. The moon was casting shadows, and before my light beam shined on the object, I saw the shape of a head sticking out of this five-foot-high snowdrift. My stomach rolled as I thought, *How could a person fly that far out of a car?* It had to have been forty-five feet away from the car. I walked, or plowed, my way through the snow to the head, and then my question was answered. When I was just a few feet away from this object, I realized that it was not the head of a person but an expressionless Styrofoam face that once held this lady's wig. It had been ejected from the car, through the back window and—*poof!*—into the snow bank it landed.

It was later discovered that this lady, to be blunt, I'll state she was fifty-eight years old, had sustained a concussion. Her sister had never even been in the car with her that night!

Roll over, Peg; I'm going back to sleep!

Performing Under Stress

♪♪♪

I would venture to say that at least eighty percent of the ambulance calls I was on were stressful. It is not an everyday occurrence to hop into your vehicle, drive fast to the nearest fire department with a blue light flashing on the top of your car and have people look at you like you're trying your best to impersonate a police officer. "Hey, Martha, look at that guy. He's flying through town with some kind of flashing light on his car. Doesn't look like an unmarked cop car, though; it has too much rust on it." When you reach the hall, all sorts of good-natured fellows are yelling at you, saying, "Quick!" (Everything is always "Quick!") "Get in the rig! It's an emergency!"

"No kidding, it's an emergency? Why do you think I was called?" I would state confrontationally, still half asleep.

By this time, your heart rate is closing in on 180/beats/minute, you're breathing rapidly, sweating profusely (even if it is winter), and you haven't even reached the location of the call yet. *I love it!* I did notice, over the years, that a person sort of gets used to this prerequisite, and your own vital signs don't escalate until you have actually reached the location of the call. Then you really start to sweat!

If I knew what the nature of the call was before I left my house, I would have enough time to plan for it. Preparing for the expected is always better than being surprised.

When I had a workable home-scanner—not the one with the coat hanger for an antenna—I could pretty much tell what was about to happen, an example being, "Hello, central control? This is [Pete's neighboring fire department]. We have a barn fire and are requesting mutual aid for their ambulance and a fire truck."

No sweat! I would be thinking as I nonchalantly strolled to my car, taking time to sip my hot cup of coffee. *Probably the boys sucked up too much of that barn fire smoke, and they'll be needing a few whiffs of oxygen! They'll need our truck to relay water, and that's all there will be to it. Should be a piece of cake*, I concluded.

So as I calmly arrived at the scene of the barn fire, I soon learned that the south barn wall had collapsed and injured half the force of their department! Besides that, someone had crashed a ten thousand gallon water tanker truck in the ditch on their way to the fire! Finally, a neighbor of the farmer saw the vast amount of smoke rolling off the top of the barn and had a heart attack while driving his tractor in a nearby field!

I surmised that it would take no less than an act of God to restore order at this scene. You just can't seem to plan for anything nowadays.

Animals

●●●

I arrived at the home of an emergency call, and I'm trying to get in the front door of the house when I hear the ten-year-old boy say, "Don't worry, mister, Killer won't hurt you. He just likes to bark." I tried to side-step Cujo's gnashing teeth as he attempted to take a chunk out of me. I make it through the door, I mean right *through the door*, and I think, *I'm safe for the moment*, only to turn around and find out his mate is an indoor only pet! She had more teeth than he did!

Deer

...

At one time in my life, I revered myself as an avid deer hunter. After trying to bag the big one for over seven years and always coming home with my drag rope empty, I decided to give up hunting. Two days after I made this decision, my wife came home and said, "Why don't you go down to the fire hall and get a few guys to help you bring home the twelve pointer that I just hit with the station wagon?" Has she no pride! But…venison at last.

Deer can pose a real danger to drivers. Their snoring is distracting, and they won't take their turn at the wheel on long trips!

Speaking of Deer Inside of Cars

♪♪♪

A friend of mine was on his way home from work one night, and I was to meet him at his dad's house. I noticed that he was running about ten minutes late when he drove up the long driveway to his father's house. As he walked in the house, he said, "I just hit a deer. I threw him in the back seat of the car and brought him home!"

I wasn't going to believe him until I actually saw the deer inside his car.

It was an old car, and this friend of mine was, let's say, not very Kosher at times.

"Well, let's go get him out of the back seat and get him cut up," his father said. He didn't doubt his son's story in the least. All three of us proceeded to walk outside. My friend had forgotten to roll up his rear window completely. The deer was in the car, had come to and was sticking his head out the window!

"Good thing he's not in the front seat, or he might have just stolen your car!" I said as I kept laughing.

"Shut up and go get me a hammer," my friend said.

Well, the deer got hit again, and the next night, we had our country version of meals on wheels.

Slinky

...

A neighbor of mine invited me in one day to ask my expert…okay, I'm exaggerating…my almost expert opinion on the safety of his newly-installed wood burning stove. "I dun figured, you bein' a furman an all that you might pick up on any dee-screpencies in my new wood-burning furstove!" he said as I arrived at his front door.

After inspecting the outside chimney, I entered his living room to assess the actual stove. I got down on my hands and knees to check underneath it to see if… "*Hey!* There's a *boa constrictor underneath your stove!*" I yelled to him from twenty-eight feet, three inches outside of the house.

This good neighbor of mine then came walking out to the sidewalk with this reptile (the snake was still laughing) wrapped around his neck. "Oh, you mean Slinky?" he said. "He's harmless." The snake was in hysterics now as it saw me shriveling up into a quivering mass of pale flesh.

I started to walk—*run*—home as I told Tarzan that if his house ever did catch on fire from an un-inspected wood-burning stove that I would help put the fire out from afar. A very long distance, as far away as possible!

Bees

...

They say that bees sense when you are afraid of them. Someone that was stung and is still afraid of bees must have made this statement.

The phone rang. It was a fireman friend of mine. "Pete, my boy was stung about fifteen times by bees, and we're on our way to the fire hall. We'll be there in two minutes."

I knew his boy, and I knew his boy was highly allergic to bee stings. I knew that any wasted time could cost this boy his life, as anaphylactic shock from bee stings will lead to respiratory arrest, and then little Johnny will have no more birthday parties!

I called the main dispatcher in the county and had him set off the tones for our department. I needed a levelheaded driver to be able to skillfully race towards the hospital, where a paramedic was already being dispatched, heading our way. My fireman friend was a driver too, but I knew he was in no condition to drive an ambulance with his son possibly dying in the back of it. My plan worked out well. A driver was at the hall when I arrived, and my friend and his son arrived thirty seconds afterwards. The boy was wheezing, and time seemed not to be on our side. Three minutes later, we met the paramedic fly car. They were called fly cars because that is what they did. He administered the drugs that paramedics are allowed to give via doctors' orders obtained over a radio. Johnny started to look better, and he had more birthday parties.

Spiders

The home that Peg and I bought from her grandmother was one-hundred and thirty-six years old at the time we made the purchase. (It came complete— Granny was included.) It listed a half an inch to the south. The house, not Granny, and it had a nice little half-inch triangular piece of paneling in the corners of each room.

Spiders ruled at this homestead. We tried everything to try to get rid of them, but they were stubborn and refused to be evicted. We killed them by the hundreds until one day I was ready to slap another one and abruptly froze in mid strike. I was quite sure that I was looking at a Brown Recluse. (El Poisonous Uno)

I never saw a Black Widow with its hour glass markings, but this Brown Recluse was a fiddle player, and I saw its design displayed on him just as plain as the nose on Pinocchio's face.

I only saw one over the nineteen years that we lived at Granny's, but that was enough to stir up those cautious feelings whenever I went into the basement or attic or the living room or the kitchen or the bedroom or.....

Horses

...

I have always been leery of horses!

As a youngster on my grandmother's farm in Dunkirk, New York, I can still remember the grin on Mr. Ed's cousin's face—"Easy now, Wilber"— just after he walked underneath that apple tree and swiped me and my two older brothers off his back.

Hee Heee Heeelp Purrr!

***

I attended a fireman's convention in Concord, New York, the year our department purchased our ambulance. At the convention, I noticed a fireman from some other department who had a very unique-looking right ear. It had a piece missing from it the size of a half dollar. You could see the three distinct teeth marks that shaped the edges of the missing piece of flesh. My medical curiosity got the best of me! I approached him and asked about his ear.

"Well, it happened back about twenty years ago," He said. "I was in the barn and reaching for a saddle that hung on the wall when all of a sudden I felt my horse Nipper nuzzling at my neck. The next thing I knew, he reached up and chomped off a hunk of my ear. That is how I lost that part of my ear, and that is how Nipper got his name. If I didn't love that horse so much, I probably would have named him RIP!"

Sleeping and the Lack of It

...

Zzzzz...

I don't know of too many occupations (voluntary or otherwise) where the person in question is required to awaken from a sound sleep, dress, drive as fast as possible and then be expected to perform his/her job in full competency under immeasurable stress other than that of fireman/ paramedic/EMT or an emergency room doctor who is working third shift on his second busy night in a row. Even then, he doesn't have to drive anywhere.

If you are seriously thinking of joining the EMT forces of America (and I hope you do), just remember that it may take months, or in my case years, to perfect the art of staying awake.

I can recall more than once—more like one-hundred twelve times—that I arrived at the fire hall and didn't have the first clue how I had gotten there, even though I had just driven three quarters of a mile to get there. The chief would say, "Pete, you could probably be more useful if you would open your eyes, and where are your glasses?"

I used my old trick of keeping a cup of coffee in one of those handy dandy car coffee-holding cups. Always at the ready in my car, I would gulp down the whole cup of coffee before reaching the hall. Then I would be at least half-awake before facing a possible life-or-death crisis.

This proved to work quite well during the spring and summer months, even into the late fall. It was a bit tedious and dangerous, I might add, chipping frozen coffee from that cup at seventy miles per hour, on snow covered roads, driving half awake, in the wintertime, to the fire hall. The dentist continues to reassure me that my missing tooth will grow back!

I, like most other voluntary EMTs, also have a full time job. I'm not trying to boast my worth as a member of the working class of America. I am trying to say that coming home from working eight or twelve hours as a Registered Nurse and looking forward to a full night's sleep was rare at best. My wife Peggy has told me that if the sound of the whistle didn't wake me up, she would let me sleep right through it. Someone else could answer it. By the way, that's why God created rookies. If the whistle continued to blow after twenty or so minutes, then she would wake me up.

It wasn't that she would lie in bed and think of the helpless hit-and-run victim lying in the ditch or the baby that was about ready to enter this world backwards that bothered her. It was, "Peter—wake up. Go answer that call and turn off the whistle so I can go back to sleep." By the way, where is my darling wife, anyways? Oh, oh, here she comes now...ouuuccchhh!

Spouse's Tolerance

...

Even though I often kid about my wonderful wife Peggy (and she lets me live to talk about it), I could not even begin to count the number of times I have been doing an activity with the family or have just sat down to eat dinner or have been doing whatever, and that whistle goes off.

Ever tried to get out of the bathtub, dry yourself, dress and be driving your car in less than thirty seconds? It's a challenge, and at times, I have forgotten more than my socks!

The whistle blows. Now the moment of truth has arrived. Do I stay home and ignore the whistle and face the wrath of my fireman buddies at the next meeting? "Oh, by the way, Pete, we were all wondering, where were you last night when that 747 crashed on Main Street and we had no EMT?"

Pause.

"Yah, six hundred and seventy-eight people died, but don't worry about it. See yah at the next whistle, huh?"

Or…do I bat my, "I'm concerned about the welfare of the entire world," eyes at her and then go off to the call?

After being in this type of business for going on twenty-six years, it is a given that I go. I would like to give just a few examples of our past trials and tribulations.

December 25, 1991. It was seven a.m. Christmas morning. We had only spent one Christmas (this one) with our newly-adopted daughter Susie, who was two and a half years old.

"Wake up, *aba*!" Susie said. "Aba" is Korean for "dad."

"Get your butt up out of that bed, or I'll break your nose. Santa broke into the house and left all kinds of wrapped up stuff under that fake tree in the libingroom," Susie said.

We adults managed to reach the libingroom without falling down the stairs, sat down, drank one sip of coffee and were about to open presents with our lovely daughter. The whistle goes off.

Knowing that our only other EMT attended the Christmas Eve Party last night and knowing he wasn't hearing anything right about then, I had to go. Peggy knew it too.

What could have been more appropriate for a Christmas Day than having a pregnancy call? It was a boy!

♪♪♪

August 1, 1995. Peggy and I were hosting the Skillman Family Reunion. My brothers and sisters had come from as far away as British Columbia, Canada, and Charleston, South Carolina, to enjoy old memories, playing horseshoes, barbequing, swimming, telling new lies and attempting to take more of my money in poker games.

We were just getting ready to get wet in our newly-installed (by yours truly) 21x42-foot, above-ground, seven-feet-deep-at-the-diving-end swimming pool. The whistle blows. I went to the call in swimming trunks, a t-shirt and gym shoes. I don't remember the call, but I do remember it cost me two hours away from my reunion.

I guess what I'm trying to relay to the reader is that if EMTing gets in your blood, you will find yourself making sacrifices elsewhere in your life. It is inevitable. I want to thank my wonderful wife Peggy for putting up with all the times that I wasn't there but instead was somewhere else, doing something for someone else. She has also made sacrifices for me to be a fireman/EMT for all these years.

The Wonder Years

***

Did you ever wonder how you have been able to reach the point in life that you're at right now? Me too! The practical odds of me even being alive right now are staggering. The guy you are about to read about also had those type of odds.

When I was young and foolish, I did a daring deed. I joined the Navy! I wanted adventure, and I wanted to see more than the three surrounding counties and the Adirondack Mountains. Yes, that was the sum of my travels at the young, tender age of nineteen. I used the experience of Mom dragging me off, hollering, kicking and screaming to that initial first-aid class as the basis of my decision to be a United States Navy Corpsman. Now, for you land lovers that are unaware of what a corpsman is, I'll explain. The job resembles that of the Army Medic, except we float! I was recently told by an old Vet who said he was there that one of the four G.I.'s sculpted in the statue of G.I.'s putting up the flag at Iwo Jima was a Navy Corpsman. Just thought I would throw that in.

After breezing through boot camp (liar), I was flown off to San Diego, California, to become a corpsman. Breezing through corps school (liar), I came home for some leave and relaxation before going out and bandaging up the world.

Being the all-American, blue-blooded US sailor that I thought I was, I, of course, had a girlfriend in every port. Yeah, me and Ricky Nelson sure were traveling *men*…oh, oh, here comes Peg again.

Okay, so this girl was from a few towns over from my parents' place, but she did send me a few letters while I was in California. Anyway, this is where the real story begins.

It was around December 15, 1975, and that winter was not extremely bad. There was some ice on the roads, but bare spots were everywhere. My new heartthrob and I were standing on the front porch of her dad's house when we noticed a Green GTO speeding down this three-lane hill that led into town.

I said, "I hope he knows there is a curve coming up soon!" *Crash!* He didn't know. "Call the police or fire department!" I yelled to her as I started to run towards the crashed car.

After running a quarter-mile down the road to the car, I saw that the car had flipped over, and it lay in a deep ditch. The wheels were still spinning. I thought, *It might start on fire*. My first plan was to turn off the engine. I jumped into the ditch and discovered that, on the other side of the car, the driver was lying on the ground with the car pinning the lower half of his body tightly to the ground. The white snow that was next to the car was being painted bright red by the blood that was spurting from his right wrist. Until this point in my life, I had not seen copious amounts of blood. My stomach was churning. This was a time before AIDS. I never gave it a second thought when I grabbed his wrist and squeezed with direct pressure on his wound. I wasn't an EMT at the time, but the first-aid course and the classes at corps school had more than trained me to stop that bleeding!

I managed to continue to hold his wrist tightly while turning off the engine. *When is help going to arrive?* I thought. What I later figured out to be eight or nine minutes but seemed like an eternity was how long it took the ambulance to arrive. I sat in the cold water and snow in that ditch holding onto his wrist and talking to him to keep him conscious. I didn't tell him any of my jokes, though. I didn't want to risk him slipping off into a coma!

I heard the sirens coming and felt help would be there soon. I could smell alcohol on the trapped man and thought it was probably helping him not to feel as much pain.

The police arrived first, and the officer called for a tow truck that was to winch the car off of my shivering, wet patient. The ambulance rolled onto the scene, and an EMT jumped into the ditch and said, "I'll take over now; you're looking pretty cold!" I felt the victim was in good hands as I crawled out of the ditch. I reached the road and then felt what I thought was a bear paw on my right shoulder. I looked up and stared right into the face of the head sheriff of the county. Being six-feet-six-inches tall gave him the edge. People of our county knew and respected this man. He said, "Nice job, Pete." I guess he knew me better than I thought he did. Must have been that parking ticket I forgot to pay.

To continue this same story eleven years later…

As I continued my passion of being an EMT, I also had to work for a living. One day while walking through the parking lot towards the hospital where I worked, I joined up walking with a coworker. I was working on the Adolescent Psychiatric Unit doing my thing while he was working on the Alcohol Rehabilitation Unit doing his thing. I sometimes would have to work briefly on his unit passing out the medications (as there was a shortage of nurses there also), and that is how we initially got acquainted.

During our walk, I told him I would see him later, around medication-passing time. After finishing the meds that night, he asked if I would like a cup of coffee, and of course I accepted. I said to him, "I'll tell you an alcohol related ambulance call I had in my earlier days if you want to hear about it."

He said, "Sure." I began telling him about the curve and the car flipping over and how I sat in that ditch for what seemed like an eternity with that guy.

After I finished telling him the whole story, he looked at me and said, "I know who that guy in the ditch was."

I quickly replied, "Who?"

Then he said, "Me!" He continued on telling me that the events of that day had changed his life. "I almost died that day, and I knew it was time for a change!" he said. "I gave up drinking and started to go to college to become an Alcohol Rehab Counselor. I never did get a chance to thank you that day for what you did; so thanks," he said. We finished our coffee and left it at that.

I'm pretty good at remembering names, but as you can probably tell, I'm not too good with faces.

Tradition and My Grandfather

···

He was known as many things: a farmer, a person to be leery of, a friend, a con artist, a horse trader and the town drunk! I guess I never did see the good side of him until long after he had left this world.

As a youth, I only remember him as the town drunk. My two older brothers Tom and Phil and I would always cut a wide path around our Grandpa Pete! He was unpredictable when he drank and was well known for saying "Get the $#*@ off my land or I'll #@!*$ give you a lesson you'll $#@!* never forget!"

Yes, he was the person I was named after. His given name was Elmer Skillman, but he was better known to most as just plain ol' Pete.

He was also known for the tricks he would play on his neighbors. As the story was told to me, he once dug up a neighbor's potatoes. He liked potatoes but not his neighbor. Grandpa Pete sold his neighbor his own potatoes the very next day!

He once volunteered to care for a friend's ducks while he and wife went on vacation. Upon their return, Grandpa Pete told them that the ducks were missing, but as a gesture of friendship, Grandpa invited them for dinner. "Sure, Pete, we would be glad to come over for dinner," he said. "By the way, Pete, what are we having for dinner?"

175

Grandpa Pete slowly and calmly replied, "Duck!"

During the days that I worked for a paid ambulance service, back in '79, I saw my grandfather in action just once!

Our ambulance was called to a funeral home where a woman was upset and was having trouble breathing. When we arrived, the woman stated she was doing better and declined to go to the hospital. My partner was busy having the woman sign off on the refusal for treatment forms when I happened to look over and I saw my Grandpa Pete standing next to the casket along with two other elderly men.

The first man looked at this dead person and wished him well on the other side. Then he placed a ten-dollar bill inside the casket. I thought this was a bit strange but I thought it must be a tradition for this type of funeral.

The second man came closer to the deceased, wished him well and placed a twenty in the casket. I swear on my grandmother's grave (Dad's side of the family), I saw my grandfather walk up to the casket and take the ten and the twenty out! Then he wrote a check for one hundred dollars, placed the check into the casket, wished the dearly departed well and thanked him for making change! If he was nothing else, he was one of a kind!

After Grandpa Pete died, I discovered the following about him. Going way back, to the 1930s or '40s, times were tough, and money was scarce. The town where Grandpa lived was very small, and the fire department was even smaller. They needed a fire truck, but the funds were low, and the bank wasn't going to give them the loan for the truck. My father told me after I had joined this very fire department that my grandfather went down to the bank and put his entire farm up for collateral! This enabled the fire department to purchase their first fire truck.

At first, I thought Dad was pulling my leg until my brother Tom showed me, many years later, a fire chief's badge from our department. This badge was known to be the first chief's badge issued by this department. It had the name of the fire department on it, "No. 1" was written on the bottom, and the badge belonged to my Grandpa Pete! I am holding it right now!

That fire truck was a MAC, and if anyone reading this book knows where that truck ended up, I sure would like to know. I want the bulldog from the hood of that truck for another keepsake from my Grandpa Pete! Phone number 1 (555) 867-5309. If Peg answers, tell her it's important!

Red Light, Green Light

...

As previously stated, I used to drive for an ambulance service. I would like to share this story with you.

We used to pull twenty-four hours on, then twenty-four hours off. They were long shifts, and if you didn't really watch your P's and Q's, you would end up not dotting your I's or crossing your T's.

The shift in mention was a rough one. During this all-day- and all-night-long shift, we must have had thirty to forty calls. I'll bet I put three hundred city miles on that rig that day, and they were all done at high speeds while running cautiously through stop signs and red lights. As all good things have to come to an end, so did this shift! Thank *god*. I got into my car and started to drive home when I noticed a town cop car following me with his lights flashing. I pulled over to the side of the road and waited for his explanation of why he was keeping me from slamming my head into my pillow. "Did you realize you went right through that red light back there?" he stated in his husky "I work from seven a.m. to three-thirty p.m. and haven't had my first cup of coffee yet" voice.

"Gee," I said, trying my hardest to sound very innocent, like Opie Taylor. "I'm an ambulance driver for "We Get There Fast" Ambulance Service, and I've been running through red lights for the last twenty-four hours. Sorry."

"Well, I'll let you go home and get some sleep for now, but be careful, and the next time try to sound like Andy or even Barney, or I'll give you a ticket for sure.

✚

EMTing Yourself

♦♦♦

I have often had the attitude that if I can take care of someone else then I should be able to take care of myself. Wrong!

Just off the record, if you are an Emergency Medical Technician and you do happen to get injured, please swallow your pride and ask for help. It will work out better in the long run.

We—Peggy and I—had our adopted daughter Susie for only a short time when I invited my only first cousin, Gibby and his fiancée, Darlene, over so they could meet her. They lived quite a distance from us, but like everyone in our family, they were also anxious to meet her.

As stated, Gibby is my only first cousin, and I wish I could tell you all about him, but that would be a whole other book in itself. I will tell you, I have always respected Gibby for turning his life around and making good of himself. His mother died when he was young, and our same grandmother helped to raise him. Gibby served in the Army during the Vietnam War as an enlisted man. He went to OCS (Officers' Candidate School) and became a helicopter pilot. He flew in Vietnam, pulling G.I.'s out of that jungle, and was never shot down. Gibby did this for a tour or two. I have always regarded him as a hero.

Getting back to Susie…Gibby and Darlene were on their way to our house, and I was hustling around trying to get everything just right. Peggy was off to a meeting or some kind of women's get-together that night, so Susie and I were sort of on our own. They arrived, and I became busy fussing with putting coats away and getting drinks ready. [I need to plug this little bit of information in for the reader at this time: Peggy and I were living in her grandmother's house and were in the process of buying it from her. Granny was in her bedroom busily reading her AARP magazine, and prior to Gibby and Darlene's arrival, I had made Granny some soup. Her house was very old, and so was everything in it, including the can opener. It was one of those hang on the wall, crank with your hand jobs. With all the excitement and being left all by my lonesome to watch and care for our new daughter, I somehow forgot to remove the top of the tin soup can from the hang on the wall, crank by hand can opener.]

Okay, so they arrive at the house and meet Susie. Darlene sat down on the floor and played with Susie, and Gib and I went to the kitchen to get coffee. He walked out into the dinning room, and I called, "Do you use cream in your coffee?" He said yes. I grabbed the gallon of milk and held it up to show him while saying, "I'll serve it fancy like Grandma used to." Doing this whole scenario, I gracefully thrust my right forearm into the can lid that I had forgotten to take out of that darn old-fashioned can opener. It sort of felt like a bump, and I didn't feel any pain (yet). As I walked through the kitchen, I kept noticing drops of blood on the floor. *Hmm*, I thought, *I wonder if the dog bit her tongue again.* I looked down at the dog and noticed the blood was spurting from my arm. I couldn't really put the two together. For blood to be spurting from my arm, it would only be logical that I first would have gotten injured, and I didn't remember getting injured. So much for logical deductions. The blood kept coming out, and I said, "Hey Gibby, can you come here for a minute?" (I felt woozy, real wooozy). Not thinking, I grabbed a dry dishcloth, not realizing that it had four million, six hundred and three germs on it! I used it to put direct pressure on the cut that I still didn't have a clue how I got. Gibby told Darlene to watch Susie so he could take me to the Emergency Room.

"We'll be back soon," he said.

On our drive to the ER, he said, "Oh, that cut is nothing. When I was in 'Nam [here we go with the War stories], I would have just sewn that up myself with a needle and thread. I felt more woozy.

The ER doctor looked at the cut. Being the suspicious sort and wondering about the possibility of foul play, he said, "So how did this cut occur?"

I proceeded to tell him, "Well, doc, do you know those old-fashioned can openers that hang on the wall, and you have to crank them by hand...?" After I finished, he looked over to the orderly, who was preparing the shots and suture tray.

He said, "Any story like that one has to be true. I don't think he could have made that up too easily. Okay, hand me the Xylocaine and 4.0 78 silk sutures."

"*Ouchhh!*"

⊕

Storms

▮▮▮

I loved to sit on our front porch with a nice cup of hot coffee, lean back, relax and watch one heck of a thunder storm come rolling right on into our little village. The lightning would start to strike, and it would start to hit closer and closer. "You better come inside before you get fried," Peggy would yell out to me from inside the house.

We had a powerful rainstorm one year, and man, did it rain. Just as I was getting out my *How to Build an Ark in Ten Easy Steps* book, I noticed a familiar sound in the air. "Yes, I do believe that is the fire whistle blowing," I mused to my darling wife. *I wouldn't keep a dog out on a night like this*, I said to myself. So, I called Wolfy, our half-Siberian Husky and half-coyote pet dog to come in as I went out.

This was to be more of a fireman call than an EMT call, although it could change in a flash, so to speak.

Lightning had downed a tree on a house, so the boys and I went to check it out.

The tree was one of those two-hundred year old jobs. It had been hit by lightning, and the top two-thirds of the tree were resting against someone's house. The house was evacuated, and plans were made to cut the tree down after the storm ended. By the way things were looking, that would be in about three months.

The rest of that night, we saw power lines go down and electric power to homes go out. Most of my night was spent waiting near a downed power line to make sure that no one drove over it. I believe the higher-ups label this one as a prevention call—i.e. preventing someone ending up looking like a French fry! I could leave and return to the hall after the power company guy came and fixed the downed electrical wire or if an EMT was needed for another call. No EMT was needed that night, so I ended up babysitting that power line most of that night. I didn't mind, as I knew that this type of prevention could also save someone's life. Besides the coffee was free!

Not all calls were as dramatic as those seen on TV, but all calls are important.

Now what kind of calls do you think we fireman guys had after all this rain fell? You're right. Flood calls

Floods

¸¸¸

I always used to dread flood calls. Not only are they dangerous, they are what I label as sneaky!

Have you ever walked down to your basement and discovered a little bit of water on the cellar floor? Have you ever walked down into a basement and observed a refrigerator floating toward you? I have.

Electricity is a major danger with flooding. As we all know from eighth grade science class, electrical current can and does travel quite well through water.

One, try relaying that information to

Two over zealous firemen that are half-awake as they are storming into someone's

Three-foot deep, water-flooded basement at

Four in the morning so they can be the one noted for saving the

Five-year-old, trapped wet cat that is hissing at them from a top of the electrical box. This is highly likely to put them

Six feet under!

Our old house was located next to a creek that was usually dryer than a first-semester term paper until the rains came.

I had a bumper crop of locust trees that grew next to that creek. I had planned on cutting them up into fence posts and acquiring some needed income for said fence posts from a good friend of mine. Well, he was a good friend until he found out that his fence posts went floating down the creek late that April night. What really made me mad is when we got a call that night to unplug the small bridge that was down the creek from my house. You got it; my locust trees were doing the plugging. Those guys just ripped them to shreds with those chain saws as I watched little pieces of my trees and any profits I had thought of float away. This was the raw version of throwing money down the drain.

Tornados

✦✦✦

While living with Peggy's grandmother in this quaint little village, she told us that our location was often referred to as Tornado Alley. I didn't fully swallow that whole story until she showed me a fifty-foot pine tree in our side yard.

"Peter, do you see where that tree looks like it stopped growing up at the top?"

"Yes," I said. Granny said "Well, that tree used to be eighty feet tall until the twister of '69 spun the top thirty feet of it right off and replanted it about a half a mile up the road.

Okay, so I believed her then.

At the time, five of the previous seven tornados to enter our county came within a half-mile of our house. I was fourteen years old in '69 and plainly remember the tornado Granny was speaking of. I saw the same twister roll through my Uncle Sherm's woods. It snapped off large maple trees as if they were matchsticks. I was in that woods at the time, trying to get as deep into a hole as I could. The tornado passed only one hundred yards away from me.

I think it was '87 or '88 before we got that kind of damage from another twister in our town. I remember a few minor injuries, but no one got seriously hurt. Toto and I...I mean Wolfy—have learned to respect tornados.

Blizzards

✔ ✔ ✔

I believe I have mentioned blizzards a time or two in this book already, but just in case you missed it, let me recap.

Southwestern New York is notorious for blizzards. I have only answered one, maybe two, calls when I forgot to put on my socks. You got it, during a blizzard. Call me overzealous, but I call it plain stupid. Brrr!

Blizzards can be very dangerous.

I wasn't on an emergency call when this happened, but it could have turned into an emergency call real quick. Mine!

I was driving home from work on the back roads, late at night. The weather was bad. Real bad! I could only see about ten feet in front of the car. It was snowing those snowflakes as big as half-dollars. I really became concerned when I noticed that the wildlife was trying to bum rides from me, even though my car was all over the road. I was creeping along at an outrageous speed— ten and a quarter miles per hour—when I turned a corner on an old country road and was greeted by one of those big maple trees that were planted when George Washington occupied the main office. The problem being that the maple tree, not George, was lying across the road, and it wasn't going to be moving anytime soon. *The weight of the snow must have brought it down!* I thought as I was frantically downshifting.

187

Have you ever watched a NASCAR race when one of those cars goes spinning down the raceway and doesn't hit anything? Well, that night, I made the qualifying run. I pulled every driving skill out of my bag of tricks to avoid hitting that tree. I slid sideways, I slid backwards, and Joey Chitwood would have been taking notes if he could have seen me driving that night. I was able to stop the car about one millimeter in front of the old maple tree.

I ended up driving an alternate route that night. It put me close to fifteen miles out of my way, but eventually I got home safely. I got home just in time to shovel out the driveway so I could park my car. Thanks Peg!

Blizzards and Curves

***

I shared the previous story with you just to warm you up for this one.

Our fire hall got a mutual aid call to a neighboring town one cold night. In fact, the town was conducting a blizzard. The plows were doing their best to clear the roads, but six inches of the fresh white stuff still lay on the road I was attempting to drive our "small" 500-gallon water tanker over. Stop laughing now. They wouldn't let me drive anything bigger.

The nickname of "Crash" Skillman seems to have followed me wherever I've gone.

We were short of men that night. Our fire department's members had the IQ of 180…if you added them all together, that is! The smart ones stayed home that night. To continue, I was driving slowly, and the chief's voice came over the radio while the entire county was listening. "Hey Pete, are you out there? Are you still on the road?"

I answered, sheepishly, "Yes." Then, speaking with authority, I said, "I'm still on the road, but I'm trying to take it easy as to keep this thing on the road." I no sooner said that when I approached the downhill S-curve that I had to navigate to reach town. Please keep in mind that I had 500 gallons of water sloshing around in back of me, and the roads were covered with snow and ice. I could only see about two feet ahead of the hood of the truck, and I didn't have on any socks. Yes, I will admit that I'm not the best truck driver in the world. (Boy that was hard to admit.) And yes, this was the infamous sockless call that somehow every fireman in my county found out about!

The truck went into a skid. Man, did I wish I were back in my nice warm bed at that moment. I slid that big truck (it was big to me at that moment) sideways right around that curve, knowing that I had to somehow straighten it out! The opposite curve was quickly coming into what view I did have…very quickly I might add. I thought, *Hey, the skid worked once, so let's try it again!*

At the time, my speed was faster than I wanted it to be, but slowing down was not an option. I was glad my Driver's Ed instructor wasn't with me; I would have failed this road test for sure. I put that truck into a sideways skid and slid around that curve just as slick as snot on a brass doorknob. What, no one ever pulled that trick on you? Well…back when I was in grade school…uh oh, here comes Peg. Quick, back to the story.

I finally arrived at the house fire that, by this time, was all but burnt to the ground, and I heard someone say, "Who let Pete drive anyway?" This fireman wasn't even from our district!

The House on the Left

Other Stupid Stuff

▪▪▪

Every fire department has at least one guy that is six-foot-seven, two hundred and eighty pounds and always has a story to tell. Ours, for picturesque speech, I'll name Bubba. Oh, by the way, when Bubba spoke, everyone listened.

Bubba had been a fireman for a long time and had lots of stories to share. This was his favorite one.

He started by saying that this incident happened about twenty years ago, and since then, the story has been told over and over and over again. Everyone in six counties knows it.

Bubba said, "I was telling my best friend Albert [probably his only friend], 'You should come up to fire practice with the rest of us guys. We're going to be burning this house and practicing putting the fire out.'"

"Won't the person get a little ticked off that you're burning his house down just for fire practice?" Albert questioned after spitting out his tobacco juice.

"Naw," Bubba said. "The old house wasn't worth anything, unlike his neighbor's eighty-thousand-dollar home, so he gave it to us to practice on. He signed it over to us to make it all legal and everything."

"Sure," Albert said as he smiled and showed off his only teeth (the two front ones) at the same time, "Sounds like fun."

Saturday morning arrived, and sure enough, the boys had the fire trucks pulled up to this house, and they were pouring gas all over the house, Bubba reported to me.

Bubba continued with his story. "'Stand back!' one of the guys in front of the house said as he threw a lit road flare into the house. The house erupted in flames. Soon the house was really cooking, and the flames were coming out the already broken windows upstairs!" Bubba stated enthusiastically. After taking a deep breath, he continued, "A car pulled into the driveway." Bubba stood up and, to accentuate his story, threw his arms up into the air and portrayed the man just arriving at the house, getting out of his car yelling, "My house is on fire!"

"The chief didn't look too good at this point," Bubba states. The chief walked over to the man and, after a few brief words, came back. He and Bubba started to laugh, and the chief said, "We burnt the wrong house. This is the house on the right!"

> The night bird sings a song of woe
> Of wrong things done so long ago,
> He saw the spark, he saw the flame
> But cannot say who was to blame,
> The night bird sings a song of woe
> Of wrong things done so long ago.

Respite Care
Personal Stuff

✔ ✔ ✔

Peggy and I have been on many adventures, and one of our adventures was called Respite Care.

We would use our home and our loving care to provide people with a chance to receive care at another place they were not accustomed to, out in the country.

These people were special needs people. The arrangement was made through an agency, and we had to go through some red tape to be certified "Respite Care Providers." After we were both CPR certified and our home was certified for this type of care, people started coming.

We provided care to the mentally handicapped and the physically challenged. We had young children with breathing problems and older people with special needs.

"We're having a person stay with us this weekend." Peggy informed me as I walked in the front door. "Okay," I replied.

We were paid for caring for these people, and after just recently adopting Susie, we found that the money came in real handy. Tricycles are expensive!

We took pride in caring for these people, and they often would request us again and again when it was their turn for this type of care.

The person arrived close to five p.m. in a wheelchair van. He was nonambulatory and looked to be quite frail. His equipment also arrived. That came in a U-Haul. He had a medical condition that required him to receive breathing treatments. *No biggy*, I thought. *Been there, done that!* We moved the gentleman into his bedroom, and I noticed right off the bat that something didn't seem right. I knew he had a medical history of breathing problems, but the reports didn't make him out to be as bad as what I was seeing.

I drove down to the fire hall and borrowed one of the stethoscopes from the rig (the red one, guys, I'll bring it back eventually) and returned home. I also relieved them of a blood pressure cuff, one of the good ones (not the old ratty looking orange one with the hole in the side!).

I obtained his vital signs and listened to his lung sounds. It was frightening! I told Peggy that she should call a head person in this agency because I was sending this guy straight to the hospital. He was not passing go, and he was not going to collect his two hundred dollars.

When Peggy called the agency, they informed us which hospital to send the man to. I rode along in the rig to the hospital with him. While in the Emergency Room, the ER doctor talked to me and found it hard to believe that this agency would send a person in that condition to a Respite House. The man was flown to Buffalo by helicopter and was placed on a breathing ventilator. He had pneumonia! The doc told me, "It's a good thing he came to your house and that you had the smarts to bring him into the hospital. Otherwise, he would have been in the morgue by morning!"

A Father's Pride and Joy

...

I love my kids. I may have mentioned it a couple thousand times already, but what the heck, what's one more time?

Peggy and I have presently adopted three foreign children and are planning to fly to Thailand to get another young lady. We first got Susanna Lynn Hei Young Skillman, a.k.a. Susie (from Seoul, Korea); then Stefan Peter Lynn Skillman (kind of catchy don't you think?) a.k.a. Stefan (from Yambol, Bulgaria). They were brought to the United States with an escort.

Peggy and I then traveled to Bangkok, Thailand, and then traveled further south to Songkhla, Thailand, to adopt Sarah Joanne Panthipa Skillman, a.k.a. Sarah. You may be asking yourself, "Self, what do all of his kids have to do with him being a Fireman/EMT?"

Answer: Everything.

I believe it was the year that I received the EMT of the Year Award when the Chief asked me if I would like to be the guy that takes a kid or two and rides in the back of the old fire truck on Memorial Day. We throw candy out to the crowd during the Memorial Day Parade. After thinking long and hard for approximately one one-millionth of a second, I replied, "You bet I would."

That year, we went to two parades, and I took Susie and Stefan with me.

Sarah was still in Thailand at that time. Our old fire truck was a 1930-something, red fire truck that had a bell that was rung by hand. It was more like a Conestoga Wagon with a motor attached. We used to go down to the fire hall, and Stefan would climb up into the old truck and pretend to drive it.

I sat the kids, facing backwards, up on the top of the cab. I stood in the back wagon-looking part and held on to both of them as we rode slowly down Main Street in the Memorial Day Parade, throwing candy to all the kids that were watching from the sidewalk. I know that I was as proud then as I believe I have ever been. Stefan, Susie, Sarah and Elisabeth (I'll tell you about Elisabeth later), I love you.

I'm sitting here waiting for another memory to pop into my head. I...okay, now I just got one!

The Disaster Plan That Was Disastrous

***

Fire meetings were always fun. They were usually held at the fire hall once a month. Getting in was the easy part. Getting back out alive was another story! Sometimes it got messy!

However, it was always the perfect excuse to get out of the house. "But honey, if I didn't go, they might make a wrong decision, like voting Homer in as a full-fledged member or, even worse, making him chief!"

She responded, "He would be a bit more exciting than the 'potbelly stove' one you have now! Okay, quit your whining, you can go. Bye!" The door shuts quickly, the car starts, and I'm gone! I never did much like watching *Scarecrow and Mrs. King* (it was on at the same time the meeting started), but don't tell Peg!

As stated earlier, we lived in the snow belt region of southwestern New York. It doesn't snow by inches there, but by feet. Buffalo didn't have much on us as far as snow was concerned.

"The topic for tonight's meeting will be the disaster plan for our village," said someone in an authoritative position.

"This should be a riot!" I said to my friend and partner in firefighting, who was sitting next to me.

The plan was fairly good, I will admit.

197

Our village had a large grocery store right next to the fire hall. Our fire hall was a large enough to comfortably hold four hundred people, five hundred if we used the cellar.

We had a large generator that looked like a mean green growling machine that we had purchased from the US Army. The generator was capable of running the electricity and heat in both the store and the fire hall, including the cellar. (Have to keep those cellar people warm too.)

"Sounds like a good plan to me," someone said. "Let's vote on it." Everyone always wanted to be the one to say, "Let's vote on it." That way they got their name written in the minutes, thus having their name documented in the fire department archives forever. Glory hounds!

The actual plan was intended to sustain the lives of the four to five hundred people in our village through a massive disaster, if one should ever happen— like a blizzard, which happened about every other week from the month of November to the end of May. It was even intended to assist with shelter when we would get an occasional tornado. Three hots and an old army cot were what was available. Occasional tornado means about every other year but not including leap year. We were not overly concerned about hurricanes, as we were at least four hundred and fifty miles from the coastline, but you never know!

So the secretary—who had a real typewriter, not one of these computer jobs like I'm forced to work with (when you hold a key down for too long you get ttthis)—was told to start typing up the disaster plan, and we would mail them out at the next meeting to get public opinion.

Scarecrow and Mrs. King was almost over; time to go home!

I had a whole month to run the disaster plan through my head. Then I got an idea!

"Hey, honey bunch, it's meeting night again, and I was wondering if..."

"Will you quiet down please? *Scarecrow and Mrs. King* is about to start! Go down to the fire hall and make all the noise you want," Peggy said lovingly.

"Bye!" The door shuts quickly, the car starts, I'm gone!

Over a month's time, the guys had felt pretty proud of themselves! They thought they had come up with the perfect disaster plan. They had been savoring the smell of this plan for thirty days and were hungry to taste its presentation to the immediate public.

The meeting started. "This meeting will now come to order. Please read the minutes of the last meeting." The minutes were read. "Now if we have no further input to this plan or further questions, we will take a motion to…" I raised my hand.

As stated, their intentions were good, but one main ingredient was left out. These geniuses forgot to add to the stew that was about ready to boil over!

I started to speak, saying, "I've been thinking this plan over [also] for a month now, and isn't it true that sixty-five percent or more of the people in this village are sixty-five years old or older?" Silence dropped in on that meeting like a heavy metal car dropping from one of those big junkyard magnets!

"Uh, yes, Pete, I believe you're correct with that statement," the fire department president said.

"Well, my only question is this." I started to smirk and said, "If we're having a blizzard, and we get the usual four or five feet of snow, just how are these older folks going to *get* to the fire hall? Most of them don't drive, and walking would be out of the question!" The metal car started its decent. I gloatingly said, "Wouldn't it be better if we asked for a list of people that would need assistance to get to the fire hall in case of a disaster?" *Crash!*

The president of the department sat there with his mouth open as far as possible. The vice-president began to look confused. The treasurer got up and went to the men's room. The secretary moved to her typewriter without being asked. Everyone started looking at everyone else, and I just continued to stand up and grin.

The next month, *Scarecrow and Mrs. King* was pre-empted, but I went to the meeting anyways. We all licked the envelopes and mailed out the new disaster plan with a separate questionnaire asking for information from anyone who would need assistance to get to the fire hall in the case of a disaster. We sent them to all the area residents in our fire district. We received a ninety-percent return on this questionnaire, and we enjoyed about a twenty-five percent increase on our annual firemen's fund drive that year.

Death on the Highway

***

This is not a funny story, it is a fact. I wish I didn't have to remember all the death I've seen on the highways in my twenty-five years as an EMT, but I do. I will not bore you with statistics but will just state that death is real; it is every day of the week, and sooner or later, it will be someone you know. I hate to be so blunt, but death is blunt. Death hurts. It hurts the ones left to carry on in life without their loved one. Can it be avoided? *Yes*, sometimes!

Don't drink and drive! Please.

When I was in school, someone once asked the question, "If a tree falls in the middle of the forest, and no one is there to hear it fall, did it really make a sound at all?"

My answer to this psychological question is, "If you make yourself available in the woods, you will hear the tree fall. If you make yourself available as an EMT, you will hear the call for help! That sound will also not go unheard."

Life in the Country

♪♪♪

The exquisite fragrance of wild flowers awakens your senses as the picturesque view becomes ingrained in your memory. You taste the strawberries you've just picked and feel the warm country sunshine radiating about your surroundings when then you hear some clodhopper like Festus Dewhaggin expound on the statement, "Don't step in those road apples, Marshall Dillon!"

I've lived in the country most of my life and, believe it or not, have chosen to do so!

Country living has its many challenges. A twenty-mile trip to the grocery store can be an endeavor larger than life itself. It is often made only every other week. You find yourself borrowing more than a cup of sugar from your neighbor; often. Sharing and caring for one another is a year-round harvest enjoyed by all.

Bull

♪♪♪

"Rescue 123, your call is at farmer McGregory's Farm. The only information we have received is that there has been a farming accident. Central dispatch out at 1200."

I knew I was going to make sure to put on my fireman's boots for this call. They will stretch all the way up to my mid-thigh. A feller has to be careful of what he's apt to step in on a farm!

I wish now that what I heard upon my arrival at the farm was, "Hey, Wilber, watch where you're swinging that shovel. Pppuuurrr!"

What I did hear upon my arrival was a sort of moan, holler and scream all mixed together. Our fire department had its own paramedic, and I am still glad that he beat me to that call.

The farming accident was all of that and more. One of the men working on the farm was in a field that held a bull...a big bull...a big bull with long horns. At that moment, one of those horns was being cut off of the dead bull's head. The other end of the horn was impaled in this man's abdomen.

My friend and cohort in healing (thought I was going to say crime, didn't ya?) was already at the scene and had the situation well under control. He had an IV going, a helicopter was en route, and the patient was being placed on a backboard with mast trouser already in place. Mast trousers are pants that are placed on a patient and then inflated like a balloon. It is not that we were trying to make the patient look like a Barnum and Baily flunky, but when the pants are inflated, they will put increased pressure on the veins and arteries in the legs and increase the patient's blood pressure.

I did very little at this call but watched and learned. I believe the reason I wanted to mention it was that, in different areas (the city, the country or something in between) the EMT will always run into unique situations sooner or later.

Life in the City

...

"Rescue 123, you have a call at 1400 Boardwalk, next to Park Place with a complaint of a woman having difficulty breathing. Central dispatcher out at 1201."

My partner and I raced to the location (Fake location. It was really Marvin Gardens) and discovered that the central dispatcher had neglected to provide us with vital information about the call.

Again, it was your typical mid-winter, twenty-eight and a half feet of snow, I haven't had a good night's sleep in a month and a half kind of call.

My partner and I climbed the forty-eight outdoor, cement, ice-covered steps (#1 forgotten item) that led to the front door. (I didn't exaggerate about the steps; not that I would exaggerate about anything in a book of this caliber.)

This fifty-or-so-year-old woman was in fact having trouble breathing and did want to go to the hospital no matter how bad the weather was outside. No, we didn't try to talk her out of going to the hospital just because it was a little bit cold outside. Just keep reading, will ya! The #2 forgotten item left out was that this lady weighed in at well over five hundred pounds. I was sure the dispatcher was still laughing as we were brainstorming on how in the h___ (that word is heck, not h___) we were going to get Twiggy down those forty-eight outside steps. "I'm not going first." I wanted to be perfectly clear to my partner. The accent was placed on "I'm." To tell you the truth, I didn't want him to go first either because he was the only partner I had for the next twelve hours.

We were stuck, and Twiggy's breathing was getting worse.

Then I got an idea. Let's call in the city fire department, and we'll use their ropes with our wire stretcher to slide her and the stretcher down the stairs.

"Rescue 123 to central dispatcher. Would you activate the city fire department to assist us at 1400 Marvin Gardens? 10-4. I bet he's not laughing now," I said.

To make a long story short, it worked. The firemen that arrived did not want to dare the steps either, so we bundled this charming obese lady up in blankets, strapped her into the wire stretcher, tied two ropes to the top of the stretcher and looped the ropes around a very large tree. I had four firemen with me at the top (I told ya I wasn't going to be at the bottom) and one brave soul guiding her down the steps. My partner and the rest of the city firemen were eagerly awaiting her arrival at the base camp. The worst part of that call was helping those city firemen rewind all that rope and listening to all their dumb EMT jokes as we drank coffee at the city fire department. One lump or two?

Life In Between

***

I sometimes wonder why some firemen would risk their lives to rescue a cat from a tree. Guys, just leave it alone. When it gets hungry, it will come down. Trust me on this one.

"Rescue 123, you have a call at the local park. A youth has climbed a tree and can't get down. Central dispatch out at 1202."

I'll climb a tree to get a kid out of it. Just don't call me Tarzan! Did I mention yet that besides my fear (dislike) of snakes, I also dislike heights? Man, was that boy ever high up in that tree. Momma!

Our department didn't have one of those fancy telescopic ladder trucks. You know what I'm talking about—the kind of truck where you plunk a guy in the basket and then push a button and watch your friend shoot up about one hundred feet in the air. Well, we didn't have one of those things, and the closest available one was too far away, so the men got together and came up with the next best idea.

"Let's get Pete to go up the tree!" they stated with much vigor and enthusiasm. Thanks a lot, guys!

The chief, who by the way outweighed me by a few pounds, said he didn't know how to climb a tree. Yeah, I'm gullible. He wanted me to tie a rope around myself! "Why? So if I fall, I'll hang myself before I hit the ground!" I stated as I laughed and ran from him with the rope in hand.

I tied the rope around my ankle to keep it out of my way while I was climbing.

This kid managed to climb about fifty-one feet, three and seven-sixteenths of an inch up this maple tree. I knew the limbs he used would not support my massive physique. That's what I get for eating Susie's Fruit Loops all the time.

I climbed slowly and didn't look down. That's what they always say in the movies. "Don't look down, Clem! Don't look…" *Thud!*

I got to within five feet of this eight-year-old tot and knew if I went any further that the boys down below—I was assuming they were still down there, as I didn't dare look—would be hauling me off to the hospital or the morgue right after these tiny branches broke.

I want to say the boy was scared stiff, but he was trembling so bad I saw the branches he was holding onto shake. *I need to use psychology, maybe even reverse psychology*, I thought, as we had to climb back down the tree. (Get it, reverse, and climb down! Oh never mind.)

"Boy, I get a little nervous being this far up a tree, how about you?"

"Yes," he said with a shaking voice. "I sure could use a hand down here to help me get down out of this tree."

Trying to use the calmest voice I could manage, I said, "Now, what I want you to do is to hold on tight with your right hand and slowly grab that branch just under your left hand."

He slowly descended towards me as I continued to distract him. Somehow, I had to gain his trust and help him develop the courage he didn't know he had. I was able to talk him into moving slowly closer down towards me step by step. *I've got him!* I thought as he set his sneaker onto my opened hand. I continued to talk him down until we were on the same branch.

I said to him, "You see this nice long rope I brought up with me? Watch how mad that fat guy gets down there when I cut off a little piece with my jackknife." I proceeded to cut off a five-foot-long piece of the rope, and I let the rest of it drop to the ground. I tightly tied this young man to myself, and we both very slowly climbed down out of that tree.

When we reached the ground, the boy's mother was there, crying and holding her arms out for him. When he was safely in her arms, I looked at the chief and said, "Next time, it's going to be your turn, Cheetah."

I haven't climbed a tree since that day, even though my shaking has subsided substantially.

Life

***

I have been the doc that has assisted with bringing four people into this world. I have been the EMT that has been with more than five hundred people leaving this world. I don't like that last number either, but a higher power is in control of it being so much higher than the first number.

My grandmother told me once when I was a child not to step on ants. Any life, however fragile it is, should be allowed to live. I have learned over the years that all life is fragile, and some lives need assistance to enable them to live their lives to the fullest.

That simple value Grandma taught to me years ago has re-enforced my values and encouraged me over the years to answer the call.

The One-Armed Fisherman

This story has to do with this book, as this one-armed fisherman was also a fireman. You didn't think I would stoop so low as to just fill this page with some silly ol' fish story now, didja?

I went fishing on Chautauqua Lake with this one-armed fisherman one day. Chautauqua Lake, by the way, is the musky fishing capital of the world. No kidding! Chautauqua Lake was the area where I grew up. Back to the fish story…I mean the story.

We didn't catch anything that day. Not even a nibble.

The next day, I told my dad that I had gone fishing with the one-armed fisherman, and Dad told me the following tale.

"They say by his account that he has caught the largest musky to ever come out of that lake!" Dad informed me.

"Really?" I answered. "How big was it?" I asked.

Dad said, "Well, I never actually saw this fish, but the one-armed fisherman told me it was this big!" as he held out his right arm horizontally and turned his head to the left!

The Do's And Don'ts of a Fireman/EMT

***

Do's...

Do go to the essentials classes before trying to become a fireman.

Do show up when the whistle blows (sober).

Do pay your yearly dues. Cheapskate!

Do respect your fellow firemen.

Do risk your life for him, if need be.

Do squirt the water on the fire before squirting it on each other.

Do yield the right of way whenever possible. Not everyone is a fireman!

Do pull your turn for radio check.

Do say that you are sorry to the chief when you back the brand new fire truck into the creek as you are trying to fill it with water!

Do put gas in the trucks and rig before you return them to the hall (on fumes).

Do listen to the policeman if he is yelling at you for running a red light.

Do study your EMT book and pass the final test.

Do learn how to sew so you can sew your new EMT patch on your fireman's jacket.

Do put a Tots Finder fireman window sticker on each one of your kids' bedroom windows.

Do take your kids to the fire hall and let them climb on the fire trucks when they are five years old so they can think they are firemen too!

Do encourage other (slackers) to join your fire department.

Do come to the fire hall Halloween party and make sure you are wearing your swimming knickers with your red suspenders.

Don'ts...

Don't show up for the last five minutes of the monthly fire meeting and say, "Guys, is there anymore Three-Alarm Chili left?"

Don't return the rig or trucks to the hall and leave them dirty. Not unless you want to get hosed down!

Don't say to the chief, "Hey, Chief, I think I'm ready to handle the position of First Assistant Chief" after only attending two of the last twenty-eight meetings.

Don't pick on the rookies (too much).

Don't hold onto the end of a two and a half-inch hose by yourself.

Don't pass a state trooper on the way to a call (even if your flashing light is bigger than his).

Don't practice your best Barney Fife impersonation while the officer is filling out your speeding ticket.

Don't play with the fire whistle after midnight.

Don't deny the chief of a good dousing when he needs it.

Don't drive a twelve-ton fire truck at ninety miles per hour in the middle of a blizzard on ice-covered roads.

Don't drive your shiny new car to the fire hall to show it off to your fire buddies, as they will think you have quit the department and are once again a civilian!

Don't hide any more marshmallow cooking sticks behind the back seat of the chief's car.

Don't ever say, "I don't think we can put this fire out."

Don't ever get caught with a pack of hotdogs at a structure fire.

Don't drink the last cup of coffee without making a fresh pot (or you'll be answering to me)!

Don't drive any equipment if you have had any alcohol within the last twenty-four hours (or you'll be answering to the cops).

Don't say, "I can't deliver a baby." It will usually deliver itself; all you have to do is catch it.

Don't tell a critically-injured patient to get out and push when the ambulance runs out of gas!

Don't enter a burning house alone; always have a hose partner.

Don't let some old-timer beat you at checkers.

Don't believe everything you hear inside of a fire hall!

Don't run from your house in the middle of winter, in the middle of a blizzard, at twenty below zero, without your socks on.

Don't drink frozen coffee quickly.

Don't leave the oxygen tank on the rig empty...*ever*!

Don't miss a meeting just to watch *Scarecrow and Mrs. King* ...*ever*!

Don't believe everything you read in this book!

Don't call female fire personnel "Fire Chicks."

Don't play with matches.

Don't wear your new fancy pair of swimming knickers to a barn fire in the middle of July and expect to be thrown into the swimming pool!

Don't have more than twelve "I'm a Fireman" bumper stickers on your car at any given time.

Don't test the siren on the rig or fire truck when a state police officer is passing you on the highway.

Don't drink more than two pots of coffee at any one sitting.

Don't leave your EMT partner stuck in two full-length leg splints during EMT practice after he drinks those two pots of coffee!

Don't borrow the fire truck to water your garden.

Don't kid around when the moment is serious.

Don't be spitting on anyone when you're at the top of the hose tower.

Don't think that someone will always work on bingo night. Do your turn.

Don't forget to buy my next book!

Don't let this opportunity pass you by. Become involved as a volunteer EMT, fireman or both. You won't regret it.

Confidentiality

...

As stated, I have never broken patient confidentiality. It has been tempting at times, though. The secrets I know could put some people away for years.

"Rescue 123, you have a call at 111 Peyton Place. Details will be given to you upon your arrival."

"This should be a good one!" I told my driver. When the dispatcher won't give you any more details, you kind of know that something's in the wind!

We arrived at this address, and all seemed calm and tranquil until we got inside the house.

"I've got a broken leg!" the twenty-some-year-old man said to me as I entered the house.

No big deal, I thought as I started my initial assessment and started to apply a leg splint.

It seems that this guy was up on the roof of the house for some unknown reason and fell off the roof and broke his leg.

On the way to the hospital, he said to me, "What is that form you are filling out?" I told him that it was our run sheet and that all the information about the call was written on it. "Is there any way that you can change the address on it?" he inquired.

"Why?" I probed, surprised.

He stated that he was a TV repairman, and the location where this accident occurred was not a location where he was supposed to be. This location was where his ex-wife was located.

Brother!

I told him, "Our records have to be correct, and if I was to falsify them in any way, I could be held liable."

"But if my present wife finds out that I was at the Peyton Place address, she will divorce me!"

I did the right thing; I gave him Uncle Louis' phone number. He's a darn good lawyer!

Back to Our Neighbors

...

I spoke once of our good neighbors and friends Joan and Royal. My dear wife Peggy told me tonight that I must write another story related to them. She doesn't know it, but I could write an encyclopedia on them. Just kidding boys, put them slingshots back in your back pockets! ... Thank you.

I feel compelled to first inform my readers of the structure of this wonderful family. Joan and Royal have five kids—four boys and one girl. The boys are Jeremiah, Joshua, Zachariah and Zebedee. I just used my spell check to see if I came close to the correct spelling of the boys' names. The computer started to have smoke rolling out of the back of it.

Their youngest child and daughter has the given name Annie. As usual, I couldn't leave well enough alone. I always call her Annie Bananie. Then she hits me.

In both my professional job and my volunteer work, I kept and still keep working hours that would spin an owl's neck. My usual is the second shift. Oftentimes it may stretch into the third shift, which may continue on to run into the first shift. Then, if I have time, I allow myself to become tired and try to sleep. I was pretty much in this frame of mind the day, evening or night that this happened.

Boy, that was a long shift! I said to myself as I slid under the covers. I told myself that I needed to sleep for no less than twelve hours. (Yeah right! Good luck!) I had no sooner entered the land of slumber than my wife Peggy woke me. She was holding one of Joan and Royal's kids in her arms. The kid was crying so loudly that Peggy said it sounded like a scream.

"Peter, check Zebedee's arm and see if it is broken!" Peggy instructed me. Peggy told me, much later (tonight to be exact) that I examined this boy's arm and concluded that he had just gotten an abrasion from his fall. The arm was not broken. Then, she tells me, I went back to sleep. I don't recall.

I do not remember any of this story! I probably was never fully awake when I assessed his injury. I wrote it all by Peggy's recollections. I totally do not ever remember it happening.

Good night. *Zzzzz.*

✚

The Typical Everyday
Run-of-the-Mill EMT/Ambulance Run

✦✦✦

I am going to *try* to explain the average ambulance run.

The whistle blows. My heartbeat quickens. I think, *Can I go to this call?* Peggy isn't home. Who's going to watch Susie? Susie was five at the time. Granny is here! "Granny, can you watch Susie so I can go to the call?"

"Yes," she replies as she puts down her AARP magazine. More thoughts: *Where are my car keys? What is the weather outside like? Do I need to put on my socks? Yes, there is a blizzard going on outside. Do I have enough gas in the car to make it to the fire hall? Is my car snowed in? Am I awake?*

These would be the usual thoughts I would think in the first five seconds after hearing the whistle blow.

I drive the half-mile or so to the fire hall with my blue light flashing on top of my car. Some cars pull over to let you pass, and some don't. I miss a parked truck, missing it by inches as I skid past it. I slide to a stop in front of the fire hall and notice that I am the only fireman that is at the hall so far. I plod through the snow to enter the hall as the fire whistle continues to scream in my ears. I turn off the whistle, key the microphone (to talk to central dispatch) and find out the location of the call. Still, no one else has come to the hall. I key the tones for the home scanners and say something like, "This

217

is Base 123 to all home receivers. We have an emergency call at the grade school, and more manpower is requested at the hall." I turn the whistle back on and listen to the whistle blow. I cannot leave until I at least have a driver to drive the rig. Someone to ride shotgun would be nice, but I have often gone on runs with just the driver.

Four minutes has passed by the time a driver finally arrives. I raise the overhead door and tell him the location of the call as I jump into the rear of the rig.

I put on the latex gloves and start to fill out the run sheet. We arrive at the school and discover the nature of the call. A forty-two-year-old woman janitor has fallen off a ladder and has broken her leg. More firemen arrive at the school, and I ask them to bring in the stretcher. I do the initial assessment of the patient. I do the ABC's. A—Airway. Is her airway open? B—Breathing. Is she or isn't she breathing, and how well is she breathing? C—Circulation. Assess her circulation. She has fallen and may have injured her neck,, so I apply a cervical collar to help stabilize her neck and head. The collar prevents the patient from turning their head from side to side. She broke her leg so I assessed her to see if I could feel her pulses in her ankle and foot. I splint her leg and take her vital signs: blood pressure, pulse, respirations and temperature.

I understand that a broken leg is painful but not life-threatening, so I instruct all the people that are helping to go easy.

We place the patient gently on a backboard and secure her with straps. We then place her on the stretcher and finally, into the ambulance. I instruct the driver to use lights and siren but not to speed, as the road conditions are terrible.

While driving to the hospital, I call the emergency room on the ambulance radio and inform them of our intent to come to their emergency room with this patient, if we don't end up in the ditch. I give them a full report of everything that we have done for this patient up to that time. I would also give them an ETA (Estimated Time of Arrival) at the emergency room. The answering Registered Nurse on the other end of the radio transmission might say 10-4 (okay), or she may give further instructions. The Emergency Room physician may want to speak to me and give instructions or doctor's orders.

Upon arrival at the ER, the patient is gently wheeled into the ER, and a full report is again given to an ER nurse. The ER nurse then signs the back page of the run sheet, which is a legal document. This signature means that the EMT is released of care of the patient and the ER has taken over the care of the patient.

The stretcher is re-made with clean sheets, blanket and pillowcase. It's loaded into the rig, and we leave the hospital as soon as possible. The quick departure helps keep the ambulance garage at the hospital empty for any other arriving ambulances. Then we head for the nearest coffee and donut shop.

I have personally made thousands of calls just like this one, and I've personally eaten thousands of donuts.

The Not-So-Typical Everyday Run-of-the-Mill EMT/Ambulance Run

...

The whistle blows. My heart beats vigorously. I ponder and know I can go to the call! Peggy is home and not out shopping. How strange! With car keys in hand and socks on my feet, I stride to my awaiting automobile. The engine fires up with authority, and I skillfully navigate on my journey to the fire hall.

Upon my arrival, I take note that today the turkey raffle is being held at the fire hall. It's congested with over two-hundred firemen and their families. My chariot awaits outside the fire hall, and a page opens the door for me to enter...the dream ends!

The over-anxious driver floors it and floods the ambulance. Smoke continues to roll from the back of the rig as we hiccup the ambulance down Main Street.

Over the radio, we hear a weather announcement: "And a good afternoon to all you skiers and snowmobile enthusiasts. You will be happy to hear that an Alberta Clipper is steadily approaching our area, and we are expecting no less than three feet of new snow. This will, of course, join our already present six feet of white fluff."

I said to the driver, "Shut that thing off; I'm depressed enough already!"

The rig skids, and we miss an eighteen-wheeler by mere inches. "Are ya awake up there, Sleepy?"

I ask nervously as it takes twenty seconds for him to respond, "Yeah!" Then he says, "Where is the call at again?"

I say, "I don't know, you were the one that talked to central! Call them back on the radio and find out."

"Oh, now I remember. It's at the skiing place," he stated after his yawn.

"Turn on the siren," I asked him.

"It is turned on!" he comments. *What's next?* I think.

We arrive at the skiing place to find that our patient is still at the top of a mountain range, and the ski patrol is bringing her down. Twenty-four minutes later, I continue to shiver and wait.

"Here they come," my driver reports to me as I look up and see the three orange-suited ski patrolmen sliding down the hill gracefully. They stop right at the back of our rig with our already wrapped up package. On the count of three, we all lift her, and I slip and fall, landing on my back. The patient teeters but makes it to the inside of the rig without further injury. The ambulance begins to roll towards the hospital when I brush the rest of the snow off of my ___. (That's arm, buddy.)

I say to my wide-eyed patient, "Hi, my name is Pete, and I'm an EMT."

The eighteen or almost eighteen-year-old-looking female looks into my eyes and says, "We…" I correct her, saying, "No, I was just talking about me, not both of us."

I then realize I may as well have been talking to a refrigerator as she is speaking French. She is one of the students who came from Toronto or Quebec or maybe even France to enjoy our ski resort. *Wonderful*, I say to myself.

I call central and let them know I am transporting what I think is a minor, without a parent, no I.D. and she only speaks French!

When the dispatcher, who is also a sheriff, replies with a 10-4, I know I heard the other guys at central laughing in the background.

As we drive towards the hospital on the quickest route, we come to a Road Closed sign and have to backtrack almost ten miles. I call central again to make them aware of our misfortune.

When he 10-4's me this time, I hear no laughter in the background, just a few suspicious *Hmms*

Just to make my life more interesting, while finishing my en-route assessment of little miss downhill racer, I happen to notice an alert bracelet that she is wearing on her left wrist. I assume it says that she is a diabetic but I am not certain of the fact because it is also in French!

My patient begins to cry, and I find it very difficult to comfort her, as my French is rustier than my car. Come to think of it, I never did take French in school.

I finally call the hospital to give them a report, and I hear more laughter in the background.

On our return trip to the fire hall, we run out of gas! I forgot my wallet and have no change to purchase any donuts!

Okay, I may have exaggerated some on that story. The siren actually did work.

The Jaws of Life

♦♦♦

I have been on the guest list for many 10-13 gatherings.

Cars are a wonderful but peculiar invention. I wonder if Mr. Ford would have continued with his invention if he had witnessed the death and destruction by automobile that I have witnessed over the years!

I have seen cars in strange places. I have seen them upside down in a pond, in creeks, in the woods, on top of one another, inside a house, and on top of a building, but they're usually next to the roadside.

When a car accident happens, many physical changes take place. Cars are made of metal, and metal bends. After the accident is over, this metal may have to be bent again to get the people out of the car.

Someone invented a wonderful tool called the Jaws of Life.

This tool's purpose is to apply pressure in two different directions. When correctly used, this tool will free otherwise trapped people from a vehicle. This tool does help save lives.

The 10-13 in the Creek

***

"Rescue 123, your call is a 10-13 on the corner of Slippery Road and Dead Man's Curve. The car is in the creek. Your time out is 1400 hours."

Whenever we got a call for a car accident, we hurried as fast as we could. Whenever we got a call for a car accident in the water, we hurried faster.

It was mid-April, and this teenager had to test his wings in his newly-acquired Firebird. This car could really fly, but it couldn't swim worth a darn.

Our rig came to a stop at the scene of the accident. I saw the car lying on its passenger side in the creek. There were about two and a half feet of fast-moving snowmelt water that April afternoon.

My partner had his portable radio with him, and I had the orange box in hand as we both ran towards the car. I looked inside and saw the teen struggling to keep his head out of the water.

"My foot is stuck, and I can't get it free!" he screamed as he looked at me in terror.

"Call for a truck, and make sure they have a Hurst tool [another name for the Jaws of Life tool] onboard!" I yelled to my partner. I entered the car and positioned myself in a manner as to allow the trapped patient to rest on my bent knees.

"We'll get you out," I reassured him as I became wetter and colder from the water splashing around me.

The impact of the car in the creek bed had somehow caused the break pedal to bend forward, and it was trapping the driver's right foot. Then, I felt the car move slightly.

Water is a powerful force, and over the years, I have learned to respect that force. I heard the trucks coming, but the car shifted again. This time it moved the car two or three feet. The water was coming in the broken rear window, and due to its new angle of entry, we were both getting very wet. *I have to keep him above the water*, I thought to myself as I saw a burly fireman open the driver's door and put the Hurst tool in place.

The car's break pedal was bent backwards. It took two more firemen to get inside of the car to lift this person out and away from his—almost—watery grave! The neck collar was placed on him after he was moved, but the priority had been to keep him from drowning first.

Our patient was taken to the closest hospital, along with his broken foot. I was taken to the changing room to put on dry clothes. It is always a thrill to walk into the donut shop with OR scrubs on.

There is no doubt in my mind that this teenage boy would have died from hypothermia or drowned that day if the Jaws of Life hadn't been used to free him from the cold water in that car that sunny April Day.

The Day the Fire Hall Caught on Fire

♦ ♦ ♦

I have often wondered what we would do if, someday, the fire hall caught on fire. One day that question was answered.

I'm not sure if yours is, but our fire hall's whistle was rigged up so that if the fire hall ever did catch on fire, the firemen would know immediately because the internal alarm system would trigger the whistle to blast up and stay up. (With a regular fire call, the whistle sounds up then down.) Is there such a thing as a regular fire call?

It was about eight a.m. when I was awoken by the whistle. Our bedroom window is almost the exact same height as fire whistle located a half-mile away on top of the fire hall. Escaping its alarm was not an option!

When I wake up, it usually takes me about a week before I am fully cognizant. So, being that I didn't respond to the whistle for a moment or two, that didn't surprise me. Then I realized the whistle was not coming down. "The fire hall is burning to the ground!" a small voice inside me shouted.

At the fire hall, three seconds later, I soon learned that I was the second fireman to the call. The first fireman was in the kitchen burning the toast that set off the internal fire alarm system. He didn't get off the hook easy!

Refresher Courses

How I used to dread refresher courses!

"Okay, boys, next week we will start our EMT refresher course, and just to give you a heads-up, they have decided to change everything that you have learned up to this point and time. Have a nice night."

It would never fail. We would go to those refresher courses every three of four years, and at least one, but usually six billon and twelve things, were changed by some bigwig who published those EMT books. I personally think that they did it to increase the sale of trousers. They had some way of knowing that, sooner or later, veteran EMTs would become too big for our britches, and we would need to buy another pair! It was either for that purpose or for the purpose of selling those $24.95 EMT books! You decide.

I think it's a dangerous practice to change too many things too quickly.

First they taught us the pre-cardial thump, and then they taught us not to use it. I went on a cardiac arrest call about a week after they told us not to thump. I almost dislocated my right shoulder stopping my descent in mid-thump, not to mention the curious looks that I got from a distraught family member!

Another change that used to frustrate me to no end was when they (the Big Boys in Albany) would change the requirement levels for EMTs doing or not doing certain procedures.

First an EMT II could start an IV, then they couldn't. Then you had to be an EMT III to insert an endotracheal tube and a paramedic to defibrillate. It eventually got to the point that I questioned whether or not I was legally covered for putting a Band-aid on somebody! I'm sure glad my uncle Louis is a good lawyer!

Patches

***

"I'm depending on you, son, to pull the family through…" I'd better stop there before I enter the plagiarism realm.

Have you ever seen a fireman's windbreaker with all those patches on it?

I knew a lot of guys that lived and breathed just to earn another patch to sew onto their fireman's jacket.

The patches are sort of an advertisement that silently state the owner has attended and successfully passed a stated course.

A standard patch may read *Interior Firefighter*, meaning this guy is crazy enough to go inside of the burning house to extinguish its flames. Total IQ requirements being 7.

They're a quarter of an inch high and three inches long. They're worn on the sleeve of the jacket. These stripes sort of reminded me of the military chevron stripes worn on the sleeves of military personnel.

I once saw a guy with so many patches I was unsure if I was suppose to salute him or not!

Just kidding, guy, stop pointing that hose at me! …*Splash!*

Honesty

***

Yup, by golly gee-willikers, I saw him take that last cup of coffee and slip out the back door of the fire hall just as slick as a whistle, without makin' another pot of coffee. Just wait 'til Pete hears 'bout this!

Honesty comes in two forms: Guilty and Not Guilty.

I was on a call once at the residence of an elderly gentleman who was in some sort of medical dilemma and in need of going to the hospital. He lived alone and was a bachelor and had been his entire life. I don't recall exactly what his medical situation was at this moment, but I do remember the money I saw in the drawer as he opened it and said, "I better take some of this with me since I'm not sure when I will be coming back."

This gentleman had one of those 1900 versions of what is known as a buffet. He had a key for the locked drawer and felt secure leaving, I'm guessing, approximately fifty thousand dollars locked behind this eighty-year-old, flimsy, rusty, you could break it open with a screwdriver, unwatched lock. My partner and I looked at each other and said at the same time, "Let's go!"

Five days later, the elderly gentleman returned to his residence, and his money was waiting there for him.

This story is true, and I can honestly say that I have been on countless calls where I, or one of my partners, could have, let's say…lightened the load. We never did!

When you are in this type of business, paid or volunteer, it is your oath to provide help to the patient in all forms. Honesty is one of those forms.

♪♪♪

Two firemen returning to the fire hall after battling a blazing barn fire for the last eight hours:

"Man, am I ever tired, Fred. I didn't think we would ever get that barn fire out!"

"Now, Barney, if you're going to act like that all the way back to the hall, then just pull over and let me drive. It wasn't our fault that Pete put the refilling hose down the gas pipe instead of the water pipe!"

My Dad Is a Fireman

I am only six years old
But that is old enough I'm told,
To know that when my dad gets home
He will eat his supper cold.

He will come right through that door
As I have seen many times before,
And throw his coat right on the floor,
Fall in that chair and begin to snore.

He will smell
Like burning smoke,
If I get too close,
Then I may choke.

I love my dad
Even though he is this way,
Down to the fire hall,
He will often stay.

He will say
He is standing by,
For another company,
I don't know why.

Sis says he helps people
That he don't even know,
He goes out in the rain,
The sleet and the snow.

Mom knows that what he does
Is ugly, dangerous and grim,
Her faith keeps her strong as she knows,
A fire angel is watching over him.

Questions with My Answers

...

Q: How old do you have to be to become a fireman or EMT?
A: Eighteen, or at least look eighteen.

Q: Do they let girls become firemen?
A: Yes!

Q: Pete, were you ever scared at being a fireman or EMT?
A: No…Yes.

Q: Pete, do you always tell the truth?
A: Don't rush me, I'm thinking.

Q: What do you do if you can't turn off the fire hall whistle?
A: Blame it on the chief.

Q: What do you do if you scratch the new fire truck when you are the one driving it?
A: Blame it on the chief.

Q: What if the chief sees you scratch the new truck?
A: Blame it on the assistant chief.

Q: How often will I have to work bingo if I join the fire department?
A: Never!

Q: Do I get to drive the $175,000, brand new fire truck?
A: No!

Q: Why?
A: Because!

Q: Pete, does your wife belong to the fire department?
A: No!

Q: Why?
A: Because she's smarter than I am!

Q: Pete, what does a 10-13 mean?
A: Does your mom let you talk that way at home?

Q: What should you do if you're driving a ten-ton fire truck on ice and you begin to skid?
A: Pray!

Q: Pete, have you ever wished you were not a fireman/EMT?
A: *No*!

Q: Pete, what do you do if the little boy dies right in front of his mother's eyes?
A: Start CPR—that will give her hope, and it will give him a good chance at living again.

Q: How many quarts of oil does it take to run a fire truck?
A: A lot.

Q: Pete, what is the best way to stay calm at a rescue call?
A: Make sure you drink all of your ice coffee before reaching the fire hall, without chipping a tooth.

Q: If you had to do it all over again, would you, Pete?
A: Yes!

Q: What is the best way to deliver a baby?
A: With your eyes open!

Q: How many firemen does it take to screw in a light bulb?
A: One, if he hasn't been drinking!

Q: Pete, what is the best advice you can give a rookie fireman/EMT?
A: Don't play checkers with anyone over the age of sixty and expect to win!

Q: Dad, have you ever been on a gory call?
A: Yes, now get back to bed!

Q: Pete, have you ever taken a patient to the wrong hospital?
A: Yes, now pass that coffee pot, will ya!

Q: Pete, have you ever gotten a cat out of a tree?
A: *No!* ...And I never will!

Q: Have you ever gotten lost on the way to an emergency call?
A: Yes, more than once!

Q: Pete, have you ever talked back to a state police officer?
A: Not loud enough that he could hear me!

Q: How many snakes can you fit in Pete's fireman boots?
A: None, if you want to see the sun rise again!

Q: Pete, how do you eat three-alarm chili?
A: With a cast iron spoon!

Q: Is it true that a paramedic is two EMTs placed end to end?
A: Yes!

Q: Pete, how fast should I drive to the fire hall to answer the call?
A: It all depends on where the nearest policeman is.

Q: Pete, does the stuffed toy dalmatian on the dashboard of the fire truck really bark at four-thirty in the morning?
A: Yes!

Q: Pete, is it true you rescued Santa out of a chimney once?
A: I'll never tell! Ho-Ho-Ho!

Q: Pete, what are the three best things in life?
A: My wife, my kids and good adhesive tape!

Yesterday

...

The Beatles sang "Yesterday." I also believe in yesterday. I believe that what I did as an Emergency Medical Technician and fireman made a big difference in many people's lives.

I'll repeat a story I once heard about a young boy walking down the beach. He saw thousands and thousands of star fish that were drying up on the scorching sand and doomed to die because they couldn't reach the life-saving water. He started to pick them up one by one and throw them back into the ocean, giving them back their life. An old man saw what the boy was doing and approached him and said, "You can't possibly think that you can save all of them, so why does it matter?" The boy picked up another starfish, threw it into the ocean and said, "It matters to that one."

I realize that in just a few places in this book, I have sort of taken the liberty to brag a little. (Yeah, more like throughout the whole book.)

I often wonder if someone else would have saved the girl that got the hole in her forehead, the two guys that flipped the car into the farmer's pond on that cold winter night or anyone in the other stories. Probably, but I will never know for sure. I do know for sure that I have changed life and death situations, and you can too! I hope you have enjoyed *911: Twenty-Five Years as an EMT*. My wish is that in twenty-five years, I will be reading your fireman/EMT book. Good luck and God bless.

Among my other hobbies, I am a Christian Rock drummer and have also spent eighteen years as a professional Registered Nurse. I have spent most of that nursing time working with children with psychiatric problems.

While I was writing this book, Peggy, my first three children and I took a side trip to Songkhla, Thailand. Peg and I adopted our fourth *and last* child.

Her name is Elisabeth Ann Kotchanan Skillman, and she is seven years old. After I teach her English, the first thing I plan on doing is having her read this book!

This Is the Last Story...I Promise

...

As all good things have to come to an end, so does this book, but not until I write one last story.

My son Stefan went to his first prom last Friday night. It was a real ball watching him get all gussied up to show off his two step moves or whatever they do nowadays. The pictures were taken, a corsage was given and pinned, and the limo driver came and off they went.

He and his lovely date were seated in the limo when, all of a sudden, there came such a clatter, and only the limo driver knew what was the matter. The limo caught fire, that is what was the matter! Not to put out the fire of this memorable evening, Stefan's date's father was—you guessed it—a fireman. Stefan, his date and three other couples who were limo-less were in need of some sort of transportation to the prom. Being the inventive sort, Stefan's date's father decided to make this a night they would not forget. He delivered them all to the appointed dancing place in a fire truck! Of course, the whistle and lights were all in full performance.

Stefan told me the following day that he will never forget his first prom or how he got there.

Let the tradition continue.

Bye for now.

-Peter Lynn Skillman, EMT, RNII HM3, Daddy X-IV

I hope you have enjoyed my little book of fireman and EMT experiences that I have lived. I'm throwing in a curveball now. To the best of my memory, all of these stories I have told you are true or fairly close to being true. Except for one. Yes, I planted a fraudulent story in between the exciting and the...well, I can't give it away now can I? You may ask why. Louder, *I can't hear you*! You will find the answer to which story was made up in my next book, entitled *The Life and Times of Peter Skillman*. Ha Ha Ha!

Or somewhere else in this book! xoxoxotherookiexoxoxo!